THE SWEETEST GOODBYE

ROADMAP TO YOUR HEART, BOOK #5

CHRISTINA LEE

To The Deepest Blue readers who wanted Billie's story. He certainly needed one. And our cute and sweet boy is definitely all grown up! You're welcome.

BILLIE

B *illie,*

I GUESS THIS IS GOODBYE. You will always be my first love. But also one of my best friends. I'll text you from Ohio as much as I can. But promise me you won't wait, even though you sounded adamant last time we talked.

I only want you to be happy. With or without me. Just live your life.

ALWAYS,
   Leo

DIDN'T MATTER how many times I read his four-year-old note, my heart still made its way up my throat and lodged itself there until

I swallowed it back down. *Just live your life.* The paper was beginning to curl around the edges, but now I kept it flattened in one of my cookbooks. The one Grammy bought me after I graduated from culinary school.

That same cookbook was in a drawer beneath the cash register in Montgomery's Sweets, the bakery I ran for my family. I didn't know why I kept it. Maybe because Leo was always fresh in my mind, the memories of us as teens riding our four wheelers out on Shady Pines Preserve in order to steal a quiet spot to kiss and touch. Quick hand jobs here and there while our mouths were locked together. And then our first time...a night I'd never forget.

"He said to be happy," Dylan drawled, motioning to the letter sticking out of the book, "not mopey or pining for what you didn't have."

Dylan was my only employee at the shop and also my best friend since high school. He'd had a pretty rough life, and my family sort of adopted him as our own. According to Grammy, he had a standing invitation to all Montgomery dinners and events.

"Shut it," I replied, placing the cookbook back in the drawer. "Stay out of my business. I get enough of that from the other Montgomerys."

I noticed the small smile that lined his lips. He liked being considered an honorary member.

"I'm just your voice of reason," he said, opening the special glass case reserved for the town of Roscoe's furry friends. He began lining the shelves with the remaining dog cookies he'd frosted this morning with all natural ingredients.

My service dog, Bullseye, gingerly made his way to the corner of the room and lay down, not even giving the freshly baked snacks a second glance. He suffered from hip dysplasia—a condition Labradors are predisposed to—so his joints must've been aching more than usual today.

He wasn't allowed in the kitchen area, but he kept close watch in the main shop like a sentry. Everyone in this small town knew by now not to pet him while he was *working*, even if he wasn't wearing his special red harness anymore.

My seizures had all but disappeared after I turned eighteen, but Bullseye still warned me on a couple of occasions over the past few years. He was a loyal companion, so it was hard to see him getting up in age.

"How about a treat, buddy?" Dylan squatted down and rubbed Bullseye's hind leg, while giving him one of our baked pet bones.

When Bullseye fished it from his fingers and wolfed it down, Dylan grinned. He loved Bullseye. *As did Leo.* Every time we texted over the years, which had boiled down to every few weeks, he asked about my dog and seemed concerned about his well-being. Supposed he should, if he was going to follow in his father's footsteps and become our town veterinarian someday.

It was a big deal for Leo to be accepted into OSU, especially if he wanted to apply for their graduate vet program afterward. They only admitted about sixty students from out of state each year. But part of me hoped he'd choose a closer university in Florida.

Fact was, Leo and I never had the opportunity to give a real relationship a good enough shot. He went away to boarding school our sophomore year and then off to college a couple of years later. We could never line up at the right time or in the right place and Dylan always said that was why I had some fantasy in my head of our ultimate reunion. He didn't know Leo as well as I did, having only moved into an apartment with his father to attend school in our district in the eleventh grade.

But what he did know of him, I didn't think he liked. Leo's family was considered affluent for our small country town and Dylan was as far from being affluent as one could get, if you considered he'd once been a homeless teen.

"Still on for tomorrow night, *Will*?" Dylan asked just as the oven dinged.

He was the only person who ever called me by my birth name, William, or shortened it to *Will*. It made me feel older, like a different version of myself, and I secretly loved when he used it. Especially when we hung out every Saturday evening, without the aid of my seizure dog.

It was the one night of the week I most looked forward to. I could let loose, even drink extra, and he'd be my designated driver, no questions asked. I had only recently gotten my license back since you needed to be seizure-free for a year in order to operate a motor vehicle. Which made me feel all kinds of dependent.

The exact reason I enjoyed manning this place on my own was because I could be whomever I pleased. I hated being pitied or babied and even though my family loved me, I still felt like a fragile and sick kid in their eyes.

"Can't wait." I wiped my hands on a kitchen towel before filling the glass sugar containers for the patrons who regularly ordered coffee.

The bakery opened in an hour and I had to show up before dawn six days a week, but I set my own pace and priorities and practically had it down to a science. Truth be told, when you added in an overprotective family, I had almost too much help. Though Dylan was definitely a lifeline. He made me feel normal, even if he did drive me bonkers.

Montgomery's Sweets was a smaller shop—only enough room for four round-tops and three stools at the counter. We normally sold out of what we baked during the week, and our sugar cane syrup was as popular as the pies, which were my specialty. Twice a week Grammy whipped up some muffins too, because she loved keeping active and helping out.

My shop had become a place where people stopped for a

breather, or to satisfy their sweet tooth after they'd been shopping in town. Just like I'd always pictured.

Dylan turned up the stereo and bopped around the counter to some hip-hop tune like he normally did. Too bad his real dream had fallen to the wayside.

"Get those dancing shoes ready, *Will*," he said, and I rolled my eyes.

2

DYLAN

Billie liked when I called him Will. He'd get this gleam in his eyes and his spine would straighten. I started doing it shortly after high school graduation. I knew he always felt coddled by his family, probably because his mom died when he was born and he'd been living with a seizure disorder. His family did tend to hover over him, but I found it endearing since I had the exact opposite experience growing up.

But I got it, Billie needed to stand on his own two feet, which is why he was so proud to open Montgomery's Sweets a couple years back. When he asked if I'd assist him I knew it was not only in an effort to help me get my life in order, but also to prove something to his dad, Grammy, and siblings. That he was all grown up and could manage something of his own.

After we stacked the glass cases with our freshly baked cookies and pies, Billie flipped the sign on the door to OPEN and I got started filling beans in the coffee machine. He was wearing those tight, dark-wash jeans again. *Christ.* Ever since Billie had finally let loose and danced down and dirty with me at Lasso a few Saturdays ago, I couldn't help seeing him in a different light.

Billie was my closest friend and the best guy I knew. He was super resilient and determined—and somewhat of a control freak —and came through a tough seizure disorder with flying colors. I admired him even in high school and secretly wanted to be part of the Montgomery family because mine had been pretty shitty.

After my drunk-ass father had found out I was gay and kicked me out on the street my senior year of high school, my dream to apply to Julliard washed down the drain like the grounds from yesterday's lattes. Outside of enjoying this gig with Billie, dancing was the only other thing I was good at. Before I was hired at Sweets I was stringing jobs together to make money, in fast-food joints and lumberyards.

But the itch to dance again outside of bars or the privacy of my own bedroom was closing in on me. And even though Billie would frown upon it—because he was wound tighter than his grandmother's jewelry box—I planned on taking a job at STUDS Friday nights in Gainesville, for extra money. It wasn't exactly stripping and the dance club had a pretty cool vibe. Unbeknownst to him, I planned on showing him just how awesome this coming Saturday.

As I lined up the mug beneath the expensive machine, I thought about how I'd do just about anything for Billie. Even ignore our touching from the other Saturday night, though it was purely innocent on his part.

Billie didn't get out much with friends—he'd always been that way, more than likely because he didn't feel he fit anywhere, especially with a therapy dog constantly at his side. He was more of a homebody and normally just played video games, tried new recipes with his grammy, or chilled with his family. But I could tell he liked our Saturday nights out. I think he felt safe with me and that meant everything. Because he provided a kind of safety net for me as well.

"I figured we'd head up to a new club," I said over my shoulder as the machine did its thing, pumping out the right amount of espresso into the cup. He was kneeling near Bullseye, obviously concerned about his beloved dog's health. That animal was the one constant in his life and I didn't want to think about what would happen when it was time to let him go.

I poured the usual vanilla concoction into his mug and made sure it was nice and frothy before I handed it to him. "Unless you want to hang out at Lasso again?"

He shrugged. "I don't care where we go. Just nice to get out of here for awhile."

"There were a couple of hot guys there last time," I said, wiggling my eyebrows for effect. "Maybe you can plan on hooking up."

I wanted him to be happy and I wasn't exactly convinced that waiting around for Leo was the right thing, no matter how honorable it was. He rolled his eyes in irritation. He didn't like hooking up, but he'd done it before—he wasn't Mother Teresa, after all.

I, on the other hand, considered a healthy sex life a normal part of being a young adult. Either that or I was hornier than my friend. Besides, I sort of needed human contact, not gonna lie.

"We'll see." He sniffed at the vanilla latte and took his first sip. His eyes closed in bliss and then he licked the whipped cream I had loaded on top especially for him. I had to look away because more than once since our dirty dancing night I had the crazy notion of tasting that pouty mouth and sticking my tongue between his lips to lick at the sweetness.

But that was a far-fetched illusion because I knew Billie didn't let anybody get that close. Allowing somebody to jerk him off after clubbing was one thing, kissing and intimacy were another. Unless your name was Leo.

That guy didn't know how lucky he had it, with Billie still pining over him years later. If he came home this summer and decided that he didn't want Billie, then he was going to break his heart and I was liable to smash his teeth in. Except Leo had never asked him to wait; the letter proved it. Billie was just that way—loyal to a fault.

So I pretended like nothing at all had happened or changed between us that Saturday evening because in reality, nothing had. To any outside observer, we were just dancing. How his fingers had dug hard into my lower back as he held onto me and his hot breaths fanned against my neck were only part of *my* fucked-up fantasy.

He was letting loose and I loved every single minute of it.

"I'll pick you up at eight."

ON SATURDAY my car rolled into Shady Pines Preserve and up to the main house that boasted a wrap-around porch. I was tired from working my first night at STUDS last night, but at least I got a nap in after my shift ended at Sweets.

The Montgomery family used to solely run a hunting preserve, which included gators, but now Billie's brother Braden handled the smaller quail and deer groups while his daddy tried his hand at sheep herding. His brother Callum had a talent for creating wood furniture and sold it out of his workshop or the furniture store in town. His sister, Cassie, who graduated from NC State, handled the business end of things.

But Grammy was the glue that kept this family together and to me she represented a kind of mother figure, like no one else ever had. She waved to me from what had become her regular seat on the porch and I made sure to climb out of the truck so she could offer me her sweet tea like always.

Billie was damn lucky to have such a supportive family, even though they drove him crazy. Cassie was married, his brother Braden was still single, as was his father. His other brother Callum was dating this super-hot guy named Dean and they had just gotten engaged.

I didn't know too many other people around here who were open like that so it was nice to see an out-and-proud gay couple, townsfolk be damned. Billie had even dragged me out to some pride event with Callum's friends Jason and Brian in the Jacksonville area last year. We had a blast and I hoped to be invited again.

Grammy patted the seat next to her on the porch swing. "Nice to see you, Dylan."

"You as well," I replied, heading up the steps. "I smell something good baking."

"My cornbread muffins," she smiled. "Waiting on the timer to tell me they're ready."

"Making extra for Sweets in the morning?"

Grammy worked with Billie every Sunday shift, and had never missed a day.

"Sure am." She poured me a glass of sweet tea from the pitcher and I took a grateful sip. It had been a hot one for a spring day. "Where are you two off to tonight?"

"The usual," I replied, careful not to say too much or Billie would get on my case. "Just kicking back with a couple of beers."

"Uh huh." There was a strange twinkle in her eye. "I'd tell you take care of my boy, but I know you always do."

I felt a blush creep across my cheeks. She'd said something similar countless times before, so why this instance would register in a different way was beyond me.

No more dirty dancing on Saturday nights. Unless it was with some other hot boy.

3

BILLIE

We were sitting on a couple of bar stools at STUDS, having just arrived an hour before. The place was something else—with its sexy dancers atop elevated platforms and a rowdy vibe—so I appreciated finding a tucked away corner with a view of the entertainment. A few people seemed to know Dylan, including the bartender, who gave him a wink, so he probably came here without me plenty of times.

Dylan was already swaying his hips like somebody had plugged him in so I must've been lame company compared to when he visited his haunts by himself. But he never made me feel boring—in fact he always seemed just as excited about Saturday nights as I did. Or maybe he was just trying to get me to act my age and not like a twenty-two-year-old curmudgeon.

We had just finished watching a drag queen performance and it reminded me of that time a couple years back when I met Leo in New York City and watched Dean's friend Tate perform at a bar called Ruby Redd's. He had hooked us up with a backstage view, since we were still underage at the time, and it was amazing.

But it was also a shitty weekend because that was when I

discovered that Leo was dating somebody new. We had no ties to each other except our history, but I was jealous and I guess I had hoped we'd be intimate during our meet up.

Regardless, we stayed with Tate and his boyfriend, Sebastian, and they showed us the city. It was incredible but also way crowded—I craved the openness of the preserve and the quiet of Roscoe. Leo and I had a good time, but there was some tension between us and we sort of had a fight. Really it was me grumbling at him and feeling needy. Damn, I was pathetic sometimes.

He'd never once invited me to visit him in Columbus and had admitted to dating several guys. I couldn't be pissed though; I had dated around too. Just not seriously or for more than one night. Guess I was always reserving a spot for him, which was a far-fetched notion, I realized. I figured when he finally earned his bachelor's degree and came home this summer before enrolling in his graduate program we could see if there was still something between us. One last shot.

If something had happened between us on our trip to the city, I'd only harp on it. Like I did with everything. I used to be way more easy-going and mischievous when I was still under my family's thumb. Christ. At what point had I turned into my brother Callum?

But who the hell was I kidding? Long-distance relationships could be brutal. When Dean had stayed in North Carolina at the beginning of their relationship, Callum had moped around a hell of a lot, that was for sure.

Besides, after living the life of a college kid, would Leo still want to be with a childhood friend born in a hick town and raised on a hunting preserve? He wasn't even certain if he was going to settle in Roscoe. But maybe he would if he wanted to be with me, like I wanted to be with him.

"C'mon," Dylan said, buzzing with the same untapped energy that always mystified me. The dance floor became packed as the deejay spun some popular '90s pop tunes. "I love this song."

"In a few." I wrenched my arm out of his. "I want to finish my drink."

"Fine." He arched his head. "By the way, the hot twink in the corner keeps checking you out."

I took a quick sweeping glance. The guy was blond and cute. "Whatever. I don't think I'm interested."

Dylan shrugged as he mouthed the words to the old school Britney song. "You have *needs*, Billie. Everybody does. Your hand can't always do the trick."

I rolled my eyes. "Of course I do. I just..."

"You're waiting on Leo," he said like it wasn't a conversation we hadn't had a million times before. Was that a tad of disappointment I detected in his voice? "You're trying to hold out until summer. Because he's coming home and you're hoping when you finally get to spend a good enough chunk of time together, he'll see the light."

Sometimes I wished he didn't know me so well. "What's wrong with that?" I squared my jaw.

"It's not wrong, *William*," he said in that parental voice that he knew grated on my nerves. "It's admirable and completely adorable."

I stared into his eyes waiting on the sarcasm, but this time none came. I didn't buy it for a minute.

"Except," he continued. "Outside of hoping you don't get hurt...I think it's okay to get your needs met. At least dance with somebody, have some fun. You used to be way more loose in high school."

There it was, the unwarranted advice.

"I *am* having fun," I bit out, and then proceeded to sip on my drink, so that I didn't start an argument. I knew Dylan had a point, but I wanted to enjoy the evening in my own way. "Stop lecturing me. Besides, letting a stranger paw me is not what I want."

"Then get your butt on the dance floor and paw all over me again."

He went there. He brought up the other night when I had let myself go with him. I did touch him like I never had before while we were dancing. It was one of the best times I'd had in recent memory. Since then I'd put it out of my head and he seemed to as well.

"No way," I said, shaking my head adamantly. "Besides, you're my best friend."

"That's the point."

"You're saying let it all hang out with somebody I know and trust." I had to raise my voice as the song changed over and people began shouting the lyrics. "Which would be you."

"Exactly," he replied, smiling over his shoulder at some guy at the edge of the dance floor.

So glad he could multi-task flirting with preaching to his friend.

Playfully nudging my elbow, he said, "You're actually fun when you don't think too hard about every damn thing."

I felt a stab of regret for the naïve and laid-back kid I used to be.

"Whatever. I did enjoy myself that one night. There, I admit it," I replied begrudgingly. "But I don't want you to get the wrong idea."

He rolled his eyes. "Dude, really? You're talking to the guy who would dance with just about anyone if it meant I got to move these hips."

His dance moves were incomparable. The way his body glided across the floor. Even though he didn't bring it up much anymore, his dream was to be classically trained at a prestigious school. He had taken some local classes at the community college, but he'd dropped out when he couldn't even pay his rent.

Besides, what future would he have with dance in this town? The one and only studio already had instructors who'd been there for years.

Shortly after I hired him, he'd talked about saving up his money and moving to a bigger city in Florida to pursue his dream. But I hadn't heard him mention it in at least a year.

"You've got a point," I quipped. "You don't care *whose* hands are on you."

Was that a flash of hurt I detected behind those narrowed eyes or I was imagining it?

He placed his hands on his hips in a challenge. "So then use your friend the slut to get your needs met."

"What? No...I didn't mean..."

"You'd rather know the person, so here I am. Just your regular fun guy, open to anything," he said through gritted teeth. "You'll know where to find me."

Dylan turned and headed into the crowd and I felt like shit that we'd argued over something so frivolous. But knowing how carefree Dylan was, he wouldn't even give it another thought or bring it up again.

The guy on the dance floor who'd smiled at him earlier stepped into his space and kissed him on the cheek. Dylan threw his arms around his shoulders and swayed his ass in a seductive manner. Maybe it was the alcohol I was imbibing in, but I found him sexy tonight.

He was also magnetic, always drawing the eye of men in the room, every place we went. Whether it was the thick and wavy hair he kept shaggy or his amber-colored eyes that were wild and kind at the same time. Maybe even that scruff on his chin or the way he smelled sort of spicy and woodsy mixed together. Well damn, apparently this wasn't the first time I was noticing these things about my friend. I had already catalogued them in my brain. What in the hell was wrong with me?

Smiley dude stepped in close behind Dylan, hands on his hips, his groin plastered to his ass as they moved together in unison. I felt an all-too-familiar tightness in my throat, a cloying kind of anger that was choking me tonight, the same and yet different from every other time I observed Dylan getting it on with somebody. I didn't like when he hooked up on our nights out—but I'd figured it was because he was like my safety net and when his attention was diverted I suddenly felt alone.

Besides, I always thought he gave too much away. He should save himself for somebody who deserved him. But those were my lofty ideals. I couldn't make him see how special he was.

As Dylan reached back and ground into smiley dude, I felt my cock stir to life. Holy fuck, I really was as hard up as Dylan made it sound. I immediately diverted my gaze to the hot men dancing in tiny shorts on the platforms. Customers were below them feeding them dollar bills. Some of the guys were touching each other for the audience and damned if that wasn't hot.

My eyes skated around the bar, looking at possible prospects, wondering if I shouldn't take Dylan's advice and find somebody to dance with, too. Besides, the last text I got from Leo, he was heading to some popular OSU club, so essentially he was doing the same thing.

I thrust the thought from my brain and focused on the cute blond in the corner who had been eyeing me earlier. Except now he was making out with some other dude who already had his hand down the back of his jeans.

I sighed as my gaze naturally drifted back over to Dylan. When our eyes met across the bar and he winked at me, my cheeks immediately caught fire. What the hell was wrong with me tonight? Why was I feeling so insanely horny right now?

Maybe because I hadn't had sex in several months. At least not good sex. I was a bottom through and through but I wouldn't allow myself to get beneath just anybody. No fucking way. Last time I tried the guy wasn't exactly gentle. It didn't help that I couldn't relax the entire time.

It took a lot to let myself go and I hadn't been able to in a good long while—probably not since Leo, which might've been the reason nobody else would do.

It wasn't like he was waiting on me, though. Fucking hell. Apparently, it was turning into an uncharacteristically strange night. Before I could reason my way through, I stood up determined to head to the dance floor and find somebody to grind against.

Maybe even Dylan. What could it hurt?

4

DYLAN

I could tell Billie was thinking hard as he finished his drink at the bar. His eyebrows always bunched together and he fished his lower lip between his teeth when he was working through something in his brain. When he finally made up his mind, he'd get this adorably determined look on his face—the same one he had now—as he headed my way.

I tried to keep my heart from bursting out of my chest and my lips in a neat straight line as his shoulders squared and his feet faltered momentarily. The guy I was dancing with had his hand possessively on my hip, but nothing really mattered except what Billie needed in that moment.

"What's up?" I shouted as he got near.

"I'm tired of being me tonight," he replied, and I saw the weariness in his eyes. The effort of always doing the right thing. Always managing his illness and being super responsible. "I just want to dance again."

I desperately wanted to be the one who helped him let loose. "So let's dance, *Will*."

He stared pointedly at the guy gripping my waist. It was a sort of annoyed possessive look that made my stomach bottom out. I liked the idea of Billie being selfish about me. I placed my hand on Billie's shoulder and jutted out my hip to shrug the guy off. "Later," I said over my shoulder to him.

He moved on easily enough to somebody else and I turned my attention back to Billie. His hands tentatively grasped onto my hips, the same way they had a couple of weeks back, and as I started to sway them, he followed my lead.

Soon enough we were grooving and laughing and sweating our butts off but having a great time. We had moved into the throng of bodies as we strutted our stuff and he actually was a really decent dancer. He'd be even better if he'd only let go of the last strand of control. He was as taut as a tightrope and even though he was having a blast I could still feel the tension rolling off of him.

We were about the same height, except I probably had an inch on him, so when I turned toward the wall and he moved up against me, I noticed for the first time that he was hard as a fence post. Holy Christ. Billie was turned on from dancing with me. He must've been freaking the fuck out inside.

But I couldn't help myself. It was as if my body was filling to the brim with desire and electric energy. I moved my hand around my back to his waist and pulled him more firmly against me so I could feel him, even if it was for a fleeting moment.

He gasped against my neck, which sent pinpricks shooting along the fine hairs on my arms and legs. When his hand left my hip to tentatively wind around my chest, my nipples felt oversensitive from his simple touch. Even the cotton material from my shirt felt too restricting.

I heard a restrained whimper from his throat as he sank his weight against me, my palm clenching against the wall as I anchored his mass. Billie wasn't a big guy in the least, but when he let go like this, he felt extra heavy.

I spun around to face him and noticed how his green eyes

were blown wide, his lips trembling, his brown hair sweaty, like he was just hanging on to his last measure of control.

If he were alone, he might've simply dug deep in his pants and jerked himself off. I had no idea why he'd be so turned on right now except that he rarely let himself rub off on anybody, so the close proximity must've done the trick.

And Christ, in that moment as we stared each other down, the music and the sweaty bodies cloaking us on all sides merely faded away. All I could zero in on was Billie's mouth. His lips looked soft and shiny wet from his tongue as he panted openly.

As my fingers gripped his waist and I yanked him toward me, I wanted to kiss him so badly. But I knew that would be crossing the line for Billie into intimate territory. This was purely about carnal need.

Instead I buried my head in his neck and drew in his scent—it was one I'd already grown familiar with, but up close and personal was even headier. Like a mix of cinnamon and vanilla from Montgomery's Sweets, I had the urge to lick him from head to heel.

I rested my lips against his throat and heard him groan as satisfaction lit all my nerve endings on fire. At least he wasn't averse to being this close to me. My hands glided up and down his spine, memorizing every muscle, touching him while I still had the chance. Before he came to his senses and backed away from me.

When my fingers cupped his ass and I pulled him firmly against me, I could feel his cock aligned with mine, and holy fuck it was thick and hard as steel. Knowing that Billie hadn't been with anybody in a long time, he must've been close to exploding point. And suddenly all I wanted was to make Billie feel good.

"Dylan, we shouldn't—" Before he could finish his thought, I flipped us around so he was the one facing the wall. With my fingers, I nudged his hips to turn toward the dark corner of the dance floor. There were couples making out on both sides of us along the perimeter of the wall so we appeared to fit right in.

"Unzip your pants, Will," I grunted against the nape of his neck, before running my nose along his hairline. A shiver quaked through his shoulders. "And tell me what you want."

"What do you mean?" Billie was hoarsely panting, his eyes shut tight.

"Stop thinking so hard," I grunted and grabbed his hand, pushing it down to the button of his pants. "Let me take care of you."

"Dylan, I...I don't need..."

"Yeah, you do. You fucking need it. *Bad,*" I growled against his neck and then sucked on his skin. He moaned and swayed. "You want to wait for Leo or do you want me to take care of you right now?"

When he began trembling, I was afraid bringing up Leo had been the wrong move, so I shifted course.

"You know I love cock," I said as I arched my groin against him. "I can make you feel good."

I figured if I just acted like my normal nonchalant self, he'd relax, and I was right. His fingers fumbled to his pants and unzipped them. Then his hands braced the wall as if in surrender and it fucking lit me up inside.

"Now tell me what you want me to do," I whispered in his ear at the same time my fingers curved over the elastic of his boxer briefs. His head sank back and he groaned in response. I knew that Billie loved oral as much as he loved to bottom, but practically never allowed it. The main reason was that he had trouble letting go with somebody that he didn't trust.

He constantly warred with himself about it, because the idea of being coddled reminded him too much of being a sick kid and not being in control of his own body.

I, on the other hand, was pretty versatile in the bedroom and I especially loved being on my knees and having a fat cock in my mouth. Not that I could do that here, but hopefully my hand would do the trick, since he was putting his faith in me at the moment.

As my fingers slid over the front of his boxers, I kissed his neck so it looked like we were just making out in a dark corner to unsuspecting patrons.

"Tell me, Will."

"This is crazy—"

"Just tell me," I rumbled.

He whimpered out his plea, finally letting go. "*Please, touch me. I need someone to touch me.*" I understood that sentiment completely.

I hummed against his ear as my fingers dipped behind the soft cotton material of his underwear. His cock was warm and fit nicely in my palm. Shorter than mine and already thick and leaking. Damn, I wished I could see it—along with his expression—when I unraveled him like a loose thread.

As I stroked him from root to tip, he panted out a harsh breath and his head fell forward, as if in relief.

"Pretend your pretty cock in is my mouth, Will," I grunted into his ear. I felt his shoulders quiver. "I'm on my knees for you. And your hands are on my head guiding me, helping me deep-throat you."

He jerked in surprise, his whole body going still for one cataclysmic moment, before his head dropped and he let out a guttural moan. His cock turned heavy as a sandbag in my hand and I figured he was seconds away.

My other hand reached beneath his shirt to tweak his nipple as I continued helping him come undone. "And I can't get enough of your cock. It's fat and just the right size for my mouth. I have no gag reflex so it's sitting way back in my throat as I suck you dry."

"Holy fucking hell," Billie blurted out as his come shot over my hand and trickled down the front of his boxers. It sucked that he'd have to go home like that, but in the end I hoped he thought it was worth it.

I held him closely against me as he panted and shuddered attempting to gain some measure of control—the same control he had given up to me. And I'd be fucking grateful every day. I got my last whiff of him, the vanilla now mixing with the scent of come, making me rock solid behind my zipper.

I kissed his skin one last time as I helped tuck him back in and zipped his pants. "Heading to the bathroom to wash my hands. I'll meet you out in my truck."

I stumbled away from him, so damn hard I could barely see straight. I got my ass into the first stall that opened and locked the door. I unzipped and yanked on my cock until I came, all the while imagining it was Billie's hand gripping me.

5

DYLAN

I tried my best not to make Billie feel strange or embarrassed on the ride home, even though the evidence of what we did still wafted in the air between us in the stuffy truck. I could tell he was sticky and uncomfortable as he shifted in the seat, but he also had a sated gleam in his eyes that I couldn't help feeling good about placing there. The musky scent of our come mixing as my fingers gripped the steering wheel made the night even more surreal.

When I pulled into Shady Pines and Billie slid out of the truck with an adorably awkward glance, he turned back to me. "Dylan, uh, thanks. I—"

"Catch you later," I replied in a chipper voice, cutting him off. I waved and continued jamming to my tunes as I headed out of the long driveway. As if we'd just been two friends taking a load off after a busy week of work.

When I got home to the basement apartment that I rented from Earl Brown, an elderly man on a pension, the air felt stifling. The place was a shithole of leftover furniture and some-times I slept on the couch because it was more comfortable than my bed, but at least I could afford the lease. No way did I ever want to sleep on the streets again. But I also didn't want to stay here forever. I was going to save my money from dancing at STUDS to get a place I could finally call my own. And maybe even go back to school.

Billie grew up with the luxury of having a place to call home and family always surrounding him, and as I lie down in my sheets, I ached with the same loneliness I always did, wishing for something I didn't have. I dried my damp eyes with the heel of my hand and told myself to suck it up. At least I had a little taste of heaven tonight. I got to put my hands on the same boy I'd been half in love with since high school. He trusted me because I made him feel safe. And that was everything.

The weekend flew by with errands and helping Mr. Brown mow the grass and weed the flowerbeds. He was too arthritic to do it himself and it came as part of the deal in renting the apartment. I was used to it though, because if I didn't keep the yard up for my dad, the neighbors would've started to complain. Say what you will about rural hick towns, but everyone took care of their own.

In fact, I'd heard my dad was evicted not long after he kicked me out and no longer lived in Roscoe. For all I knew, he was conning another unsuspecting woman out of her money, like I heard he did my mother, whom I never met. Apparently she skipped town a few months after I was born.

I hadn't seen Billie since I dropped him off Saturday night. Since Grammy worked with him every Sunday, and the shop was closed on Mondays, it was Tuesday by the time I laid eyes on him again.

But I made sure to waltz into Montgomery's Sweets like what happened between us in that dark corner of the bar was no big thing. No way I wanted it to be awkward between us day in and day out. It took Billie several hours to relax around me, but then we simply fell into the same routine, which was definitely for the best. He tried bringing up the topic a couple of times, but I didn't want his guilt or his apology, so I kept brushing him off.

"Let sleeping dogs lie," I hissed at him. Eventually he gave up, but given the kind of guy he was, I knew he stewed on it for the rest of the afternoon.

Still, I couldn't shake the feel of my hand around his cock all week long. I had regular hookups so it should've been no big thing, but it seemed every time he passed by me on his way to the mixer to beat the egg whites for our lemon meringue pies, all the hairs on my arms would be buzzing. One time I heard him inhale sharply through his nose as our hips brushed, but I couldn't go there. Not with him. If I did, I'd be the one left hurt and disappointed. So I just chalked it up to one nice fantasy.

On Friday, I showed up at STUDS for my usual shift. Same as last week, I was dancing beside this guy named Aaron and I'd admit it was awesome to get my groove back on. Up here above the crowd I could be anybody I wanted to be. I could pretend I was in some show where people paid to see me dance. And not just with tips—like the bills hanging from my waistband tonight —from men who got close enough when I bent low on the platform.

Tonight we were blinged out with some top hats and suspenders and the audience ate it up. The closet in the back changing room had different props we could use to help make our little corner of the bar interesting.

Aaron was an awesome dancer and we were able to get in sync during certain songs so it looked like we had rehearsed it. I was beginning to look forward to Friday nights. Like all of my stressors of the week could be washed away just from being pumped up on my own adrenaline. I felt like I was the king of the world instead of a minimum-wage dancer in a nightclub.

"You've got some great moves, Dylan," Aaron shouted over his shoulder as he shook his ass in my direction. The club shorts we were given to wear with the STUDS logo on the back were tight and showed off our bulges well. But Aaron's ass was perfection and gave me something to focus on—especially on nights like this when my thoughts and emotions were all over the map. "Have you ever been in a dance or theatre troupe? Or did you train somewhere?"

I wished my answer were different, but if it were would I seriously be dancing in this type of club?

"Nah, I was never able to make college work or a dance career, for that matter," I said and then rolled my eyes. "Obviously."

"Don't sell yourself short. Hey, listen." He slinked over to me and threw his arms around my shoulders so we could talk and coordinate our dance moves. "I belong to the Sunflower Community Theatre in Gainesville. We have a production coming up —*Hairspray*," he said, his eyes lighting up.

Holy fuck, it was as if he knew my list of top five musicals of all time. Not that I ever had the money to see any of them. But I watched a bunch of stuff online.

"You should audition just for the hell of it," he continued, pretending to nuzzle my ear. "You got a decent singing voice?"

"I guess so," I replied in a daze, because a thrill shot through me right along with panic. I certainly didn't want to get my hopes up, because I also would probably be way too rusty for them. Besides the fact that I had no resume to speak of. "But I wouldn't be able to carry a tune solo."

"We're only trying to fill in the background dancers and you'd join in the chorus. Have you ever been in a theater production?"

I thought of how often my father and I had been evicted and how many different school systems I'd been in. A couple of them had show choirs I'd joined. But that seemed ages ago. "Not many and definitely not as an adult."

"No worries, we're not Broadway or anything. But we do have a ton of fun." He shot me a wicked grin and then grabbed my hips to grind us together as our audience below cheered. "When we get back to the dressing room, I'll give you the information.

All you have to do is come up with a two minute original audition number."

For the first time in a long while, I felt a different kind of buzzing in my stomach—one filled with possibilities.

"Now kiss me, so we get more tips." He grabbed my head and fused our mouths together as the crowd went wild. His lips were rough and when his hands grabbed my ass, my cock got stiff. But like most of my hookups, it was purely a physical sensation. My heart was never in it—probably because it already belonged to one smart, sexy, and driven boy.

If Billie ended up with Leo I would wish them well, and hopefully someday I'd find a guy to call my own. But definitely not tonight.

The following Saturday, Billie and I went out like clockwork. I briefly wondered if he'd come up with an excuse to bow out, but as he sank into the passenger seat of my truck and we drove to Lasso, he acted just as glad to be out as always.

Lasso was a bar we had frequented on a couple other occasions and a place he would've considered safer—since there was a miniscule dance floor fueled solely by a honkytonk jukebox.

As Billie found us two bar stools to sink down on, I realized how relieved I was that we weren't at a loud and showy dance club tonight. Truth be told, I was pretty tired—it had been a long week.

But as I looked him over I felt a wash of disappointment too. More than likely Billie and I would never mention what happened between us again. But at least we were back to our normal routine.

6

BILLIE

My brother Callum was shooting the breeze with Dylan up front. It was after our lunch rush and I was busy restocking some of our inventory that had sold out in a flurry.

"I can't believe you're getting married," I heard Dylan say.

"Right?" Callum replied, squatting down to pet Bullseye. He was lying near the main window, his favorite perch to watch the town, while still keeping an eye on me, of course. I almost felt guilty, like I should relieve him of his duties and allow him to rest peacefully like a normal aging dog would. But Dylan reminded me that I was Bullseye's favorite human on earth and that he'd follow me everywhere I went, regardless.

"It's about time," I said, lifting a tray of oatmeal chocolate chip cookies.

Callum had popped the question a few months back, apparently while he and Dean were visiting Gus near the apple orchard. Gus was our resident albino peacock that only made an appearance after midnight. There had been some sort of inside joke between them for years about Gus—one I wasn't sure I wanted to know—so it seemed fitting that the bird was witness to their engagement.

In lieu of a bridal shower, Grammy was holding what she called a *grooms' luncheon* on late Sunday afternoon after Sweets closed up shop. Guests were expected to bring the men gifts for the new home they were building on the property.

Callum had been living in a small trailer that Daddy had helped him construct a few years ago near the orchard, but Dean couldn't deal—he needed more room, he'd said. To hell with tiny houses. He'd been commuting to his university job at the lab and would still keep his apartment there, but the house was Callum's wedding gift to Dean.

And Grammy wanted to fill it with all kinds of stuff.

"Grammy put you up to making all the dessert?" Callum asked, standing to his full height. He was like a giant ginger lumberjack, and was even taller than our brother Braden. We didn't even seem related. I had always been on the thinner side. My brown hair was a lighter shade than Braden's, whereas Callum and my sister, Cassie, had the same auburn hair as the photos I'd seen of my mother.

"Nah, I volunteered," I replied. Besides, I wouldn't trust anybody else with the task. Unless of course it was Grammy. Or Dylan, using my recipes. "I'll start baking Saturday once we close up shop. Grammy and Braden can help with anything Sunday morning after we open Sweets. Plenty of time to be ready for the afternoon."

Dylan was busy cleaning the empty glass displays with vinegar and water and I noticed how Callum stopped to whisper something in his direction before waving as he went out the door. My family always did that—conspired behind my back like I wasn't there. More than likely Callum had asked Dylan to keep an eye on me or to make sure I wasn't working too hard.

"So Saturday night is off, then?" Dylan asked, barely making eye contact. Was that a hint of disappointment I detected in his voice? Or was he embarrassed that I had caught him colluding with my brother? He knew how much I hated being babied. We'd argued about it before, but he always reminded me that he never had that growing up, so he thought it was sweet. I always backed down because he was right, but enough was enough.

"Guess so. I need to make several pies and one large cake," I said, trying to keep my own tone intact. Saturday was the one day of the week I looked forward to most. "Have fun without me."

"Nah, I'll stick around to help," he said through a yawn. He'd been looking more tired lately and I had to wonder if he was getting enough sleep.

"You don't need to." More than likely Callum had put him up to it, but I couldn't be sure. Besides, Dylan was always trying to help whenever he could. "You're not on the schedule."

"I want to," he said, rubbing out a stubborn spot on the glass. "Besides, it's for Callum and Dean. So I'll help however I can. Okay, boss?"

My nostrils flared. His tone reminded me of the words he whispered in my ear that one night. *Tell me what you want.* I hadn't been able to let go like that in a long time and he knew it —knew me almost too well.

I couldn't even look him in the eye on the ride home after I had lost myself so completely to his touch. But it was fucking nice not to have to think for a change. Having Dylan around took the pressure off because I trusted him—he was as close to me as any family member. Which is why what happened between us also felt wrong, even though it was so damn hot.

Even though it shouldn't have, it sort of pissed me off that he was so nonchalant about it. Like me making myself vulnerable in front of him was no big thing, when he knew damn well that it was. Unless I had misjudged him or as I long suspected, he viewed sex way differently. It seemed he could totally disengage from the act.

I was being ridiculous, though. Wasn't his carefree attitude exactly what I would've wanted after making that sort of impulsive decision with my best friend? A best friend that I wasn't interested in dating but was absolutely terrified of losing?

By the time Saturday morning rolled around, there were shadows beneath Dylan's eyes, which convinced me that he was either getting laid or had insomnia.

"Late night?" I asked, trying not to sound too paternal. Normally, Dylan was like an open book so for him to neglect telling me about every facet of his life confused me. In fact, he had become a bit closed off since that one night between us. And I didn't know what that meant, only that it unnerved me.

"Something like that," he mumbled and then got working at the Cimbali machine, roasting our morning coffees. Some days I didn't know what I'd do without him, without this routine of having my best friend in my life on a daily basis. I knew eventually this arrangement would have to end, especially since his passion was absolutely not Montgomery's Sweets. He enjoyed the work, but let's face it, he didn't plan menus in his head like I did every night. But working side by side with him was something I looked forward to, even if he was a pain in my ass most of the time.

"Did you have a hookup?" I asked and then cringed at myself for prying.

Why was it any of my business anyway? He'd hooked up with plenty of men over the years, so why would I care this time? It might've had something to do with imagining his hand stroking my cock perfectly, talking dirty in my ear. Did he do that with all the men he slept with? Of course he did—it wasn't like Dylan jacking me off in the corner of a night club was special.

Dylan yawned at the coffee machine and rubbed his eyes as he balanced the cup beneath, the one he always used special for me. "I don't kiss and tell."

His voice was rough and throaty much like the tone he used that night. *Imagine that I'm on my knees for you.*

"The fuck you don't," I huffed after finally swallowing the boulder wedged in my throat. "You love sharing all that shit."

"Well, whatever, not in the mood." He raised his arm and waved me off. Normally he engaged wholeheartedly in our playful bickering. "Maybe after a strong cup."

"Way to avoid the question," I grumbled recognizing that we had crossed over into new territory. And shit, that wasn't good. I needed to calm it down and stop acting like a bratty scorned lover or something.

Usually I wanted him to shut the hell up when he talked too much, even though I secretly enjoyed it. It was better than his silence. But after that one night, I couldn't help scrutinizing his every move.

"You're just a ball of energy this morning," he muttered.

"Please, you give me shit all the time." I pushed open the bakery window and adjusted the Danishes that had shifted. "So when I do it to you, you can't take the heat."

"You know what? Fine. Fuck it," he huffed. Squaring his shoulders, he took a deep breath, and looked me in the eye. "I've been working at a club every Friday night and by the time we cash out, it's late. So excuse me for needing to get adjusted to the new schedule."

I felt my jaw drop open, as if he'd told me he had signed up with the foreign legion or something. "What kind of club?"

"I...I work at STUDS." My skin felt prickly, my throat tight as if I couldn't suck in enough air.

So the night he took me there, was that some sort of a test?

"Why didn't you tell me?" My voice peaked. I was being an idiot. "That one Saturday..." The night I couldn't get out of my head.

"I had just started working there and I knew you'd act this way," he said all flustered. "So I wanted to show you that it was a cool club. Not some skanky hole in the wall."

He handed me my mug of coffee and I blew on it attempting

to get myself under control. "And don't worry, it's not like I want to quit working at Sweets. I just need extra money. And...to do something for *me*."

I was not his keeper and the fact that he guessed I'd overreact and be overprotective was not good. Didn't I hate when my own family treated me that way?

I needed to calm my butt down and be the good friend that I always was. "I'm being an ass. It's cool, I get it. I just hate when you keep things from me."

He rolled his eyes. "Uh huh."

"So tell me about the new job. What do you do?" I already knew the answer, but I asked it anyway. No way he'd be a barback or bouncer at the club.

"I dance, like the men you saw up on those huge platforms. I like it because you can sort of put on a mini-show." He had a certain gleam in his eye and that's when I knew he had found the thing he was looking for—at least temporarily. He couldn't get that at Sweets. So I needed to stop being a pouting asshole and start being happy for him. I was his best friend, not his warden. He was one of the most important people in my life.

I tried to picture him in tiny shorts, strutting his stuff and making the customers salivate. I bet he got good tips, which was great, because he could use the money.

Taking a long sip of my coffee, I savored the flavor. He had added extra vanilla for me. The shit. Making me feel extra bad. "You look beat. No need to stay tonight; I can handle it."

"Just shut the fuck up and let's get started with our day," he replied flipping the sign on the door to OPEN. "You know I'm going to stay no matter what."

I turned away so he couldn't see the immediate relief on my face. His dedication was like a salve for my soul.

7

DYLAN

W e'd had a steady stream of customers all day, but I could feel the tension radiating off Billie ever since I told him that I danced at STUDS. He'd always acted like some super responsible older brother, even though we were the same age. I wasn't sure if it was just in his blood or if it was because he's had to deal with being sick his whole childhood. Or maybe because he had to make up for his momma dying and leaving all those kids to his dad and Grammy when he was born.

I'd never say it out loud, but by now I knew what he was thinking—that I could do better. Part of me wanted to ball up my fists and tell him to go fuck himself because despite his hardships, he had some things a hell of a lot better than me. The other part of me wanted to grab him and squeeze the stuffing out of him because he was the only person in my life to give a shit about me.

To take me in, listen to me, care about my well-being...and that meant the world to me. I knew he was only concerned and meant well. So I also knew that he would get over himself soon enough.

I flipped the sign to CLOSED and locked the door. Bullseye

was close to snoozing near the entrance, one of the only things he ever did lately, besides keeping his eye on Billie and eating every treat in sight. I could hear Billie clattering away in the kitchen as I put the chairs up on the tables and finished sweeping the floor.

Digging out my smartphone, I scrolled to a music station. If we were going to finish making the pies and the surprise cake Billie had consulted with Grammy about, we needed some upbeat tunes. The best thing I could do was help Billie as much as I could because it wasn't good for his disorder if he was stressed. Even worse if he got too little sleep, which is what his brother Callum had reminded me about the other day, when he asked if I'd be staying late as well. He didn't even have to say the words—just the crook of his eyebrow did the trick.

I would've stayed anyway, regardless of whether he asked me to or not. Though I knew Bullseye was trained for added protection, the dog was getting up in age and had trouble moving fast enough or keeping his eyes open for very long. His time as a service dog was pretty much past. But he was part of the Montgomery family and no way Billie was ready to face that fact yet.

The last time he'd had a seizure was a couple of years back when Billie had been restless and upset after his New York City trip to meet Leo. He'd found out that he was dating somebody else and even though he acted like it was no big thing, I knew he was losing sleep—along with his mind. We were just getting Sweets up and running at the time, and had stayed well past midnight to paint the walls when Bullseye started whining like crazy.

I had never heard anything like it before. But Billie understood immediately, as did Callum, who was on the other side of the room. Billie lay down on the floor to soften his fall and Bullseye was right there to keep him contained with the mass of his body, so that he didn't hurt himself when the seizure came.

I had felt so helpless watching him thrash around like that, his eyes rolled back in his head. But Callum assured me it would all be over in a couple minutes' time. When Billie came to he was in a fog and spoke a few garbled words that didn't make sense. But at least I now knew what to expect.

Heading to the cupboard below the cash register, I dug out a bottle of red wine, Billie's favorite. Country boy had some expensive tastes. His cell was laying on the counter and I lifted it to bring it along. Grammy worried if he didn't respond right away.

My fingers accidentally brushed over the home button and the display lit up. I couldn't help noticing the last screen he'd been scrolling through. It was a text exchange between him and Leo from a few days ago. I knew I shouldn't read it, but I couldn't seem to stop myself.

Billie: Too bad you can't make it. I'll tell Callum and Dean you send your best.

Leo: Wish I could. A break would be nice after such a tough semester.

Billie: We'll make up for it this summer.

Leo: Looking forward to it. It'll be nice to catch up with old friends.

I sighed. If only Leo realized how much Billie had banked on his words. I was afraid he was in for a world of hurt and I was liable to rearrange somebody's too-perfect face.

I walked into the kitchen just as Billie was pulling some pies out of the oven and it smelled divine. "I swear you make the best key lime in all of Florida."

There was a twinkle in his eye and that's how I knew he liked my compliment. "Because you've been in every county in the state?"

I cocked an eyebrow. "I've crossed over more county lines than you have."

Using the hot pads, I watched as he gingerly placed a pie on the countertop.

"At least I've left the state," he said with a snort.

He had me there. Traveling was expensive and normally I couldn't do more than string together enough dollars to pay my food and rent. But I had gotten in my truck to drive around Florida, just itching to see what else was out there.

"You know I'm only messing with you," he said and the earlier disappointment about my new job was gone, replaced with the easy smile of my best friend. "We should totally take a trip someday. Remember our plans to drive cross-country?"

Back in high school, we'd cruise the four wheelers around the preserve and shoot clay targets at the wobble deck where the quail hunters practiced. Afterward, we'd lie in the orchard staring up at the sky and dreaming. Billie used to love stargazing, but there'd been little time for that lately.

Billie would probably always be a resident of Roscoe, because his family was here, but he did want to travel and see more of the world, same as me.

I figured I'd just go where the money was. I no longer had any ties to anybody in this town, except maybe the Montgomery family. I never knew my mother, and my father had disowned me long ago. He acted like my being gay was worse than him getting drunk and high every weekend. Passing judgment even though he had plenty of shit to be judged about. Too bad child services never caught up with his ass.

"I remember." I placed a new trivet on the counter so he could set down another pie from the oven. "I still want to see the Grand Canyon and San Francisco. Or maybe head east to New York and Maine."

"Maybe we should make a real plan," he said, but I knew it was only talk. He had the shop to run and plus he was probably holding out hope that the kind of trip we were discussing would take place with Leo, not me.

"Sure, let's map it out sometime," I replied, eager to agree so we could move on. No use getting my hopes up anyway. It wasn't like I was rolling in the dough at the moment. One of us had to stay levelheaded, after all.

I headed over to the cakes that were cooling on a rack, and

gently tapped the middle of the chocolate one to be sure it was ready to be frosted. They were Callum and Dean's favorite flavors and Billie planned on making each tier to their liking.

When I hadn't heard him move or respond, I looked behind me. "What?"

"You don't take me seriously, do you?" he asked, his brows knitting together. "About a road trip together?"

"I don't know. There's always plenty going on," I replied, shrugging. Then I got busy making the frosting, attempting to avoid his probing eyes. "Besides if you and Leo ever..."

"This has nothing to do with me and Leo. Anyway, he's traveled plenty," he said, gritting his teeth. "This is about you and me."

I couldn't help the small thrill that shot through me at his words, followed quickly by guilt for reading that text exchange.

Billie stared me down until I broke. "Okay, fine."

What the hell was that about anyway?

As we began decorating each layer of cake, I opened the wine bottle and reached for some goblets in order to pour us a hearty serving.

I raised the glass in a toast. "To our future travel plans."

"That's more like it." He clinked my glass and took a huge sip, savoring it as it went down.

I tried not to stare at how the wine stained his lips red or imagine how tangy they might taste. More than likely I would never know how he tasted. It was hard enough knowing how he smelled. *Fuck.*

"Okay, I'll frost one in buttercream and one in chocolate," I said after downing my first glass of wine. I'd acquired a taste for red over the years, so Billie tried to stock our favorite brand for times like these. "What's next?"

"After I decorate the tiers, I need to make a couple of apple pies. Then I'm all set." I looked around at our ingredients and began pulling out the flour and sugar containers. I knew the routine well and reckoned Billie was grateful for that. To train somebody else would be time-consuming, so I was glad to stick around for as long as I was needed. "I made a couple of crusts after the lunch rush, but I need the apples cored and sliced."

We set to work on separate tasks and before we knew it the cake was decorated, the apple pies were baking, and the wine bottle was empty.

I had opened a second Cabernet after I tossed the apples in lemon to stave off bruising. Billie was on his third glass, with sweat dripping down his temples from the heat of the ovens.

I figured while we waited, it was time to liven things up.

8

BILLIE

When I heard Dylan turn his iPod up in the main room, a smile lined my lips. Music always had to be playing in some capacity or he'd get restless. I knew he enjoyed working here, but staying in on a Saturday night to bake was probably pushing it.

Earlier, I had watched as Dylan expertly frosted both cakes for the grooms' luncheon. Whether he realized it or not, he had developed a skill. He could walk into any other baker's kitchen in the state and get a job. I knew it wasn't his passion, but he sure did take pride in it.

But what he enjoyed most about working at Sweets was being up front with the customers while I was fine hiding in the kitchen. He loved to chatter away with everyone in town, even though some of these folks had shunned him and his dad back in the day. And fuck, he deserved so much better than that.

He acted so carefree, but deep down I knew Dylan needed to feel like he mattered, like he belonged somewhere. Still he didn't like feeling dependent on anybody or accepting handouts. Grammy had even suggested he live on our property a couple years back, but he outright refused.

I left the kitchen to watch him from the doorway. Dylan's back was to me and he swayed his hips to a catchy rap tune, completely uninhibited in the empty room.

Sweets at night was a different experience. It was dead quiet in town and with the shades drawn on the windows it almost seemed eerie and clandestine. I pictured Dylan dancing exactly like he was now except in broad daylight in front of the passersby and felt a blush crawl across my cheeks.

He'd have put on quite a show and I'd suspect most of the girls in town would faint on the spot. For all the times they snubbed their noses at him in school, when he'd show up with holey clothes and worn shoes—now I suspected some came inside the shop just to get an eyeful of how handsome he'd turned out. Either that or because of the rumors of two faggots running a bakery. But by and large our business had been steady and the customers respectful.

"Are those some of your moves from STUDS?" I asked, more than curious about his new gig.

My question startled him, so when he turned, Dylan's cheeks were a bit pink. But he kept moving, never one to be ashamed of his dancing. Every time I thought about his dad throwing him out on the street and his dream of Julliard washing down the drain, I felt a stab of anger seize my chest. When I was in NYC, we had passed the famed college and I almost bought him a sweatshirt, but it might've burned too much.

"Not really," he replied, squatting down low with a sensual grinding motion as the tempo changed to another song. My cock stirred to life in my pants. I pushed down on the offending body part with the heel of my hand, wondering what the hell was wrong with me. But no doubt, Dylan's moves were erotic as sin, especially to a guy like me who hadn't had sex in ages. "I kind of just make it up as I go along. Sometimes Aaron and I play around with a couple of props."

"What kind of props?" I asked as a swell of irritation surged through me. It was one thing to dance alone but quite another to grind on someone else. I though back to our night at STUDS and vaguely remembered some of those dancers being in groups of two or threes, simulating sexy acts. Blood rushing to my ears, I reached for one of the chairs from a table and dragged it across the floor to sit down. Bullseye's one ear pricked up and then he turned his attention to Dylan's dancing as well. "Show me."

Dylan stopped mid-motion as his eyebrows scrunched together. "Show you what?"

"How you dance for the customers," I replied, suddenly blinded by the way his hips were gyrating and how his messy hair was falling in his eyes. "What do you wear? Do they stuff money in your pants?"

"What the fuck is wrong with you?" Dylan asked, his mouth curving downward. "Are you drunk?"

"Nothing's wrong," I replied, attempting to get my raging hard-on under control. All he had to do was look down at my lap to see what I was attempting to hide. "We're waiting for the pies to finish baking, you've got music on and I like watching you dance."

His eyes sprang to mine in a mix of surprise and confusion. Had I confessed too much?

"Is that right?" he asked in a skeptical voice. "Or are you just checking up on me? I don't care if you approve of my job or not."

"Yeah, you do. Just like I care what you think about my choices." His eyes flared with an emotion I couldn't quite tack down. "You're always grumbling that I'm uptight and too much of a prude."

"Because you are," he said not skipping a beat when the music changed to a different rhythm. "You don't let yourself have enough fun."

"Touché." I shrugged and leaned forward, challenge in my gaze. "So this prude is asking you to show me your moves."

"Okay, fine." He reached for his cell on the table and changed the station to a slower tempo. "You want a show? I'll give you a show."

And fuck if his words didn't make a spark of electricity zing straight through me.

Dylan began swaying his hips seductively as he inched closer to me and then suddenly his knees were touching mine flush against the chair. "There's this act we do with a stool. Aaron sits down and I dance for him, like we're in a go-go club."

He walked forward and straddled the chair, his thighs sinking down on top of my lap. His ass rested near my groin and my dick strained from the friction.

"I..." I could barely get the words out let alone inhale properly. "I bet customers go crazy. You're so..."

"What?" he asked, genuine curiosity in his eyes, along with something else. Unmistakable desire. Holy shit, he was just as turned on. *Don't look at his cock.*

"I'm sure you know how sexy you are when you dance," I panted as his eyes snagged on my mouth. His gaze lazily traveled up to my eyes as if he needed to see if I was teasing. A wash of color crept from his neck all the way to his cheeks.

"Have you and Aaron ever..." I didn't want to know, yet I did at the same time, because the idea of it was really fucking hot— even though it made my chest feel so tight, I could scarcely breathe.

"No," he replied, his arms swinging while his upper torso twisted with the tempo. "Besides, it's just for show."

I felt my jaw harden. "But if you're doing all of this to him, he's probably really hot for you."

"Doubt it," he said in a huff and then drew his hips away from my lap. "It's none of your business anyway."

"My bad." I was trembling with need and had the urge to grab onto his waist and bring him back my way, savor the pressure from his muscles and tight ass. I liked feeling the warmth of his body near mine. Plus, he smelled all musky and spicy and it reminded me of the night he sucked on my skin.

"I was just trying to...imagine it," I replied instead of what I really wanted to say, which was something about keeping away from Aaron. Pathetic. I had no idea why it suddenly mattered to me what Dylan did with other men. But what he was doing to me right this moment? Holy crap. "Living vicariously through you."

Suddenly he was right there again, our knees touching. He leaned over, his eyes on me, his lips heading straight for my mouth. At the last second, he made a detour to my neck. I nearly whimpered out loud.

"You never know, one night he might say the right thing and I'll want to hook up." He whispered this against my ear and I grabbed his hips to hold him at bay, to keep him from sinking down on my cock, which was about ready to explode.

I knew my fingers were trembling against his waist. "Wh... what kinds of things?"

"I don't know. How about you tell me?" He sucked my earlobe into his mouth and I just about melted into a puddle on the floor. I groaned, imagining how his mouth might feel against mine— his tongue. But I reminded myself that I didn't go around kissing anybody. I was reserving my lips for Leo.

Except Leo was the furthest thing from my mind right now.

"If you were up on the platform dancing with somebody sexy," he breathed against my throat as his hips swayed back and forth. My grip tightened on his hips. "And were really horny, what would you say to them?"

"What?" My brain was foggy as Dylan sucked at a spot on my neck and he was going to leave a mark if he didn't cut that shit out.

"We're just pretending, right?" Dylan asked, leaning his head back, his eyes meeting mine. "Isn't that what this is, *Will*? It's Saturday night and we're just having a good time?"

I nodded numbly. Yet, I felt the words form in my mouth. The ones I would never say out loud because he was just having fun and playing a game.

This doesn't feel like pretending.

I cleared my throat and sat up straighter. "I'd tell him to take off his shirt so I could admire his chest."

Dylan's eyes flared with desire as he reached for the hem of his shirt and lifted it above his head. I'd seen Dylan's bare torso dozens of times over the years. He had a lean dancer's physique. But his biceps and chest were more muscular than mine from keeping active and fit.

"Like this?" Dylan asked, his pupils blown wide. As my gaze scaled down his torso, I noticed how his nipples were hard as erasers. Pebbled brown discs that I longed to touch. We were pretending, so that's exactly what I did. I reached up with my thumb and swiped it around his areola. Dylan let out a surprised gasp before he threw his head back and groaned. It was the sexiest damn thing I'd seen in a long time.

My hand moved to my cock and I pushed down to keep from coming all over myself. "Then I'd have him turn around," I murmured, my lips trembling. "I'd want to see his back muscles while he shakes his ass."

Dylan's eyes fixed on mine as he slowly lifted one leg from my lap and spun around to face away from me. His back was bare and his smooth skin was glistening with sweat. He began moving his hips back and forth and his cheeks looked perfect in those tight jeans. *Fuck.* My cock stiffened painfully and I needed relief so damn bad. His ass was in my face and all I could think about was getting a look at his round globes and his tight pink hole.

All at once he sank those perfect cheeks down on my lap and leaned back flush against my chest. My throat released a guttural moan, overwhelmed with so many different sensations at once. I wanted to grab him around the chest and hold him to me, kiss him, make him feel good. *Holy fuck where did that come from?*

"You're tense as a rope, but I know you're turned on." His

voice was raspy and his chest was heaving. I kept my hands down at my sides, but I desperately wanted to encircle him, play with his nipples, suck on his neck. "I just want you to let go, Will. What else would you tell the sexy dancer?"

"I...I don't know." He was creating a fantasy for me, and I didn't know what to do with that. He was my best buddy and I wanted him so damn much in that moment. It scared the shit out of me because I didn't want us to go too far and kill our friend-ship. *What if we could never recover from this?*

But then I remembered his hand job the other night and how he showed up at Sweets like nothing ever happened so more than likely this didn't mean anything. It was only fun and games.

Dylan began gyrating his hips and then his shins hit the floor and he sank down on the ground in front of me. When he twisted frontward, he glanced up at me with those long eyelashes, his cheeks dotted with crimson and I didn't think I'd seen him look more attractive. "You like having someone on their knees for you?"

"Goddamn," I gasped, as his hands brushed over my shins to my thighs.

"It's hard for you to let go. To give yourself to somebody." His fingers stretched to my zipper and he roughly palmed me. "You need someone to take charge, to suck your aching cock."

I nearly sprang out of my skin. *Fuck.* "God...yes."

Were we still pretending? I didn't even know anymore.

"You know how much I like cock, *Will.*" He unbuttoned my pants and I lifted my hips to allow him more room to slide the material down. My dick sprang free and Dylan groaned. He licked his lips and stared intently at my shaft—which was purple and leaking—as if it was a delicacy.

The words were right there on the tip of my tongue to tell him to stop. But my brain had gone on vacation. Besides, this was Dylan. The only other guy besides Leo who made me feel safe.

"You have about five seconds to tell me to stop."

I opened my mouth, but nothing came out. Instead, my fingers gripped the chair tighter, the anticipation too damn much.

When he leaned forward and buried his nose in the hair at my crotch and took a deep whiff, a whimper sprang from my throat. He hummed as he lifted his eyes to meet mine and kept them pinned to me as his tongue circled my crown. It was the sexiest damn thing and I was already completely gone. Lost to him. Holy fucking hell, his mouth was warm and wet and it felt like nirvana as he suckled the head.

"Taste so good," he said as his tongue bathed up and down the length of my cock, as if cherishing it. "You like that?"

"Fuck." I adjusted my legs to get more comfortable and allow him more room. "I love it."

"Put your hands in my hair and show me how much."

Damn, I mouthed. When I lifted my fingers and brushed across his cheeks he sucked in a breath. My hands burrowed in his soft dark hair and as I gripped his locks, he engulfed my cock with his mouth. "Guhhhhhh."

I tried not to push down or thrust up, even though I knew he'd probably like that. I just wanted to savor this feeling before I lost my load, which was going to be in about sixty seconds flat.

He held onto my cock with one hand and hollowed his cheek. When I heard him unzipping himself, probably to get some needed relief, I gripped his hair even tighter, trying to maintain control for longer.

Dylan's eyes were glazed over and I could tell he was completely loving every minute of this. He always joked how much he liked sucking cock, I just never thought he'd ever be sucking mine.

I wished I could see what he was doing to his own dick, but that would've been too much. But I felt the sensation of him stroking up and down in time with his mouth. His tongue circled and laved and when he thrust down and I hit the back of his throat, I was done for.

"Jesus. That's just—" My legs turned to rubber and fireworks shot up my spine as I blasted my load into his mouth. I was quivering and melting against the seat and I heard a deep groan from his throat as he apparently came as well. I was dead weight, unable to stop shuddering as he kept my cock in his mouth long after I was depleted.

"Fuck," he whispered after another minute, as my softened dick slid from his lips. "So damn hot."

I tried to move my lips but nothing came out. Instead we stared at each other across the few inches of space between us as he tucked himself back in. He licked his lips and I imagined leaning forward and tasting myself on him. Feeling his tongue in my mouth.

The bell on the oven dinged right then, and he stood up on wobbly legs. I snapped out of my fog and began tucking and zipping.

"I'll pull the pies out of the oven," Dylan muttered.

After he left the room, I looked down on the floor and saw how his come had dripped and pooled where he knelt. I numbly stood up and reached behind the counter for some napkins to clean it up, fascinated by the amount. Wondering how it would taste. I needed to snap the hell out of it.

I heard the back door open and close and when I headed back to the kitchen, the pies were resting on the counter and Dylan was gone.

9

BILLIE

The chairs were already lined at the three outdoor tables in the field behind our house and still Dylan hadn't arrived. He usually showed up early to important family events and asked how he could help—not that he needed to.

"Where's Dylan?" Grammy asked as she straightened one of the seat cushions that she had expertly tied to each chair. She'd had countless parties and dinners on our property over the years and practically had it down to a science. We'd basically fall apart without her. At least I would. She was the only mom I had ever known.

That fact was plain to me, and even though she had no visible medical ailments, that didn't mean that she wasn't getting older or moving slower in recent years. Same as Bullseye, who was keeping watch over me on the porch—in between naps. Loyal through and through. I should be so lucky to have such devotion.

I shrugged, my mind drifting back to Grammy's inquiry and the one friend who had always stood by me. "He should be here soon."

I wouldn't mention that I had already sent him a text this

morning while opening Sweets with Braden and he hadn't responded. Sweets stayed open until noon and then Braden and I transported the pies and cake home. I didn't need Dylan's help, but he usually checked in with me. It was already two o'clock in the afternoon.

My gut tightened at the idea that he might've regretted what happened between us last night. Just imagining his wet mouth on me, the way his tongue slicked over my cock, his eyes glazed over with desire, made my stomach flip over. I forced that thought from my brain so that I didn't sport a chub in front of my own grandmother.

I flinched when I felt Grammy's hand on my back. "Something happen between you two?"

No way she could've known how intimate we'd gotten last night, so I squared my shoulders and took a deep breath. Still, I couldn't meet her gaze. "Not sure what you mean."

She grasped for my chin and forced me to look at her.

"Not sure I believe you," she said, studying my eyes. I had the urge to yank out of her grasp but I'd get a whack to the back of my neck from any one of the men in this family. You didn't disrespect Grammy. "You've had your share of squabbles, but you always make up. 'Course it's because you think you're different. Don't realize you're actually more alike. Just look at Dean and Callum."

She finally loosened her grip and I was able to back a distance away to reach for the linen tablecloths Grammy always used for these occasions.

"Dylan can be a pain in my ass," I said as if I had to prove her statement was false. "He's always in my business."

"Just like you're always in his," she said with a smirk. *Darn her.* "He's been a dedicated friend and doesn't let you get away with much."

"Yeah," I admitted, my shoulders drooping. "You're right."

There was no argument there. My stomach convulsed at the very idea of losing him.

After my sister, Cassie, showed up with her husband, Dermot, and we secured the tablecloths, I helped Grammy carry out the place settings for each guest, which consisted of a small group of family and friends who had been supportive of Dean and Callum over the years. That included Tate and Sebastian, Jason and Brian, along with Dean's parents and his half-brother, Felix, who belonged to a motorcycle club. Sounded like it was straight out of some film noir. Too bad he had to cancel last minute.

"It's a shame Leo couldn't make it. Have you heard from him lately?" Grammy asked and this time kept her opinions to herself. She knew that we were each other's firsts but also witnessed us growing apart over the years. I figured we had drifted only because we've never had the opportunity to be in the same town for very long. If we were ever given a fair chance, maybe we'd see that we really were meant to be together.

"He had to work over spring break. His last year of college has been busy," I added, to make it seem reasonable. And it definitely was. Long distance for this many years was difficult enough as a friendship, let alone a relationship. "But he'll be home this summer after graduation."

"I'm sure his family is proud," Grammy remarked, placing the napkin holder on the table while I set the small sets of salt and pepper shakers in everyone's reach. "I just never liked you waiting on that boy."

"What?" I froze in place, the last container in my grasp. She hadn't shared her thoughts on the topic in a long while. "I'm not. Not *really*."

She wouldn't think so if she saw what I was up to last night.

"I know he was your first love," she said, as her eyes softened. "But most times there's a first love and a *last* love."

"She's right you know," I heard Callum remark behind me. When I turned he was chomping on a Macintosh apple from our orchard, the juice running down his chin and almost making a mess on his perfectly starched white shirt.

I narrowed my eyes at him. *Way to have my back, brother.*

"Or sometimes—if you give it enough time—things can work out," Dean supplied, with a smile and a wink. He always tried to bridge the gap when things were heading adrift with the Montgomerys. He leaned closer to my ear, his striped tie swinging forward as if it were conspiring as well. "But Dylan's pretty gorgeous too."

My spine stiffened and I felt my cheeks heating up. "We're only friends."

"I know. Only messing with you," he said out of earshot of Grammy and Callum. He was the first person who had guessed my crush on Leo years back.

"But he sure cleans up nice," he observed, nudging me.

I followed his line of sight to where Dylan was exiting his truck. He wore a light-blue button-down shirt, nicely pressed gray cotton pants; even his hair was gelled back in a type of pompadour that might've rivaled Dean's. I never told him he needed to dress up, especially in this Florida heat, and not on his limited budget.

Honestly, I had never seen Dylan look so handsome before, except maybe at high school graduation. But he had borrowed a shirt and tie from my closet back then and certainly these clothes seemed newer.

I attempted to get my tongue unstuck from the roof of my mouth to greet my best friend properly.

10

DYLAN

I'd actually gone out and purchased some decent clothes from a second-hand shop in Gainesville because all I owned were holey jeans and T-shirts. But nobody needed to know that, most of all Billie. Thing was, even though I'd been invited to many Montgomery events over the years, most were backyard BBQ types and since Callum getting hitched was a huge deal to this family, I needed to step up my game.

"There's my handsome boy," Grammy called from the porch and I nearly blushed. I could feel Billie's gaze on me and I wondered exactly what he saw. Especially after last night. Holy fuck, what a game changer that had been.

I was sure that Billie was working overtime to come up with something super rational. We had started off pretending, or at least he did. But what we did wasn't sensible at all—just plain hot. The way his fingers tightened in my hair when his cock was down my throat. Christ.

But I needed to pull it together and tell myself that we were both just filling a need. Plain and simple. I didn't want Billie to feel uncomfortable around me. Not today.

As soon as our gazes locked, the air became thick with

tension. Neither of us seemed to know what to say or do. I figured I had to step up and offer comic relief. It was always that way. I swiped my hands down my shirt. "At least I still remembered how to iron."

Billie cracked a smile and stepped closer. "You missed a spot," he quipped and pointed at my sleeve.

"Well, it happens when you're in a rush and your best friend keeps texting you wondering where in the hell you are," I replied as if I was completely flustered when in fact it was endearing. "I didn't realize how damn needy you were."

He chuckled, as color rose to his cheeks. "You bastard. It was only once."

My eyebrow shot up. "*Twice.*"

"Sorry. I was just trying to...you left last night and—" There it was, the apology. The regret. *Sorry I got so carried away last night.*

He swallowed thickly and continued. "Besides, of course I need you. Who the hell is going to tell me whether or not my cake topping looks centered or whether I over or underdressed?"

I almost responded with, *How about Leo?* But that would've been juvenile. What he was describing was what friends did, not lovers.

Why couldn't it be both?

Instead, I rolled my eyes. "Show me the cake."

After Billie and I went inside and I reassured him that all the pastries as well as what he was wearing looked fine—more than fine—the guests began arriving.

Grammy had a mix of family and friends at each setting. But at the main table she had arranged Dean and Callum at the head, beside Mr. Montgomery and Dean's folks. Cassie was also seated there with Dermot. Braden and his new girlfriend were at one of the other tables, along with Billie and me, as if we were a matched set.

Callum and Dean were wearing the sashes that Grammy supplied that read, *Groom* and their friends got a kick out of it. Dean quipped that he needed Tate's crown, but Tate kept it planted firmly on his head, atop his purple hair. I couldn't help staring at Tate and his boyfriend, Sebastian, in his finely tailored suit, because they seemed so worldly and I just felt like a hick, even in my nicer duds.

Mr. Montgomery was a man of few words, so when he stood and made a toast to Callum and Dean's happiness, Grammy, Billie and his siblings seemed equally surprised and choked up. Billie dipped his head maybe making a silent wish that his daddy would be as accepting of him. It was something he'd struggled with his entire life—winning his father's approval.

Afterward, I could tell Grammy needed all the extra hands she could get, so Billie and I helped serve the salads as well as the main course of chicken, fish, and venison, fresh from the preserve.

It was nearly dusk by the time the gifts were opened and the delicious cake—with two groomsmen on top—was served. I finally sat down to enjoy a slice of Billie's pie, making small talk with Tate and Sebastian in the process. I really enjoyed them and almost wished I had been the one to visit the city with Billie. But at the time, the idea of it felt bitter in my mouth. I should've known Leo would disappoint him.

Once we helped clear the tables and most of the guests had left, the remaining family and friends stayed to visit on the porch with some sweet tea and Dermot's homemade wine—which tasted more like strong moonshine.

Braden had gone down to the fire pit to get a good blaze started and soon enough, Callum, Dean, Jason, and Brian had joined him. The rest of the guests made their way toward the flames as if entranced and Billie played some classic rock tunes on the stereo, which made for the perfect background on this warm and relaxing night. I was grateful to be part of it, like I had been so many times before.

I sat beside Sebastian and Billie was on the other side of Tate, and when I caught Dean's gaze across the fire he smiled in a lazy sort of way. He looked so content to be part of this family, even though Billie had shared the story countless times of how he and Callum were like oil and vinegar when they first met.

"So Billie mentioned when he stayed with us in the city that you had hoped to attend Julliard?" Sebastian asked in a hushed voice. Billie had mentioned me on his trip to meet Leo in New York City? I guess it made sense, but it still surprised me.

My gaze darted to Billie and away, as he spoke animatedly to Callum's friend Jason. "That's right. Unfortunately, my dad decided being gay didn't fit his alcoholic lifestyle, so he kicked me out on my ass to fend for myself."

I couldn't help the bitterness that seeped from my lips remembering the endless string of nights in shelters, on friends' couches, or in barns and haylofts. But this was neither the time nor place to have such a discussion. There was a long pause where I held my breath and Sebastian seemed to consider my words. "Not sure if Callum ever mentioned it, but I was homeless once too."

I numbly shook my head because that information shocked me. Afraid I had brought up a terrible time in his life I opened my mouth to change the subject, but before I could do so he added, "Thank God we're both survivors."

I had never seen myself in quite that light, but I guess he was right. I had done what was necessary to earn a meager living and find a place to live. Billie and his family had helped a ton and I owed them a lot. But Sebastian seemed so much more than that in his fancy clothes such a long way from his worldly lifestyle. I wasn't even on the same playing field with my basement apartment and pseudo-career.

"So what now?" Sebastian asked. "If that was your dream, do you still dance?"

My cheeks immediately grew hot as shame attempted to take

hold. But I tamped it down. "I...uh, dance at a club. Best I could do around here."

"I get it," he replied in a warm voice and I wondered just what he'd had to do in his life to get by.

"But this guy at work—Aaron—he also belongs to a community theatre and he told me to audition for this musical they have coming up." I didn't know why I brought it up except that I was excited and wanted to prove to him, and maybe to myself, that I was working toward something. "So I've been putting together a two minute dance routine for next week."

When I looked up Billie's wide eyes were fixed on me. "How come you never told me that?"

"If you'd get over the fact that I dance for horny men who stick dollar bills in my shorts," I motioned with my hands, forgetting myself and where I was in that moment, "maybe I would've told you."

The whole circle around the fire grew silent. *Well, fuck.* I averted my eyes because I did *not* want to see Grammy's reaction. Thankfully, Tate was there to break the tension. "I think I've found my soul twin. Why haven't you told me more about him, Billie? He's perfect."

Billie blushed furiously while I stared at the dirt and toed at some stones. A minute later, everybody returned to whatever conversation they were having, my outburst forgotten.

We hung out until close to midnight and the first to head to bed were Grammy and Mr. Montgomery. Jason was looking a bit drunk and drowsy and I figured they would be next to leave the festivities.

"Thanks for all of your help, Dylan," Grammy said in my ear and then kissed the top of my head. "You should stay in one of the spare rooms, like old times."

I didn't know how many countless nights I ended up on this property trying to make it through high school graduation and not eat out of a trash can, but I'd be eternally grateful.

"Maybe I will." I knew that I wouldn't, but I didn't want her to fret about me getting home so late after a long day and a few drinks.

At least somebody worried about me. I avoided Billie's questioning gaze.

As Tate and Sebastian said their goodbyes, they hugged me, and Sebastian told Billie to bring me along for a visit. "Or come by yourself. You're always welcome." Tate looked pointedly at me and winked, as if aware of some secret I wasn't privy to.

We helped Dean and Callum transport some of their gifts to their new home near Callum's workshop, closer to the road. It still needed some finishing touches, but damned if I wouldn't mind living there in a heartbeat.

"Want to go visit Gus?" Billie asked after we said our goodnights.

"Sure," I replied, glad we were acting back to normal after everything that had transpired between us in the past twenty-four hours. We walked to the field near the orchard and sat down in the grass by a large oak tree waiting to see if Gus would grace us with an appearance. The night air was cool, and the stars looked brilliant. Billie didn't follow astronomy quite as much as he did as a kid, but every now and again, I'd overhear him and Dean discussing space-time continuum or some shit. Dean worked in a science lab at the university and I supposed Billie could've gone either way, but baking had won out.

"Dylan," Billie began as he fidgeted with his hands. "I...I don't want you to think...I *want* you to be able to tell me things. I'm sorry I've been a shit."

"Nah." I lay back in the cool grass so I could get a better view of the sky. "I overreacted. It's all cool."

"I just—I hope you know I believe in you and I want you to be happy," he said, leaning back to lie alongside me, as Bullseye rested his head on Billie's thigh. "Do whatever you have to do to make that happen. Even if you have to leave me, too."

My breath caught as I met his gaze. "You drama king. Leave you? Please."

"Could happen, you never know," he mumbled, his cheeks growing pink, before he finally relaxed beside me.

We lay in silence for several long minutes, just breathing the same air and lost in our own thoughts. The stark truth of Billie's confession reminded me how fragile his heart had remained despite all the blessings surrounding him.

Little did he know mine was even more breakable. One more gust of wind and it might collapse like a house of cards. I couldn't dream of leaving him and I wondered if that blinding devotion had become my biggest weakness.

"I'm tired. Grammy mentioned me crashing in Callum's old room." I sat up and rubbed my eyes. "You cool with that?"

"Of course." It was late as we made our way back to the house; the only light tracking our path came from the kitchen entryway and I couldn't wait to be facedown in some cool sheets.

Cassie and her husband had retreated to her childhood bedroom, which was the first door on the left. When we turned to Callum's old room across the hall, Billie jiggled the handle, but the lock was secured and we heard voices behind the wall.

"Think maybe Jason and Brian stayed over?" Billie whispered. "He did seem a bit sloshed."

"Probably," I said around a yawn. I turned toward the kitchen to make my way out to my truck. "S'okay. The drive isn't far."

"Don't be ridiculous," Billie scolded and then grabbed my arm. "C'mon."

He half dragged me down the hall and swung open the door to his bedroom. "It's not like you've never slept here before. Let's go to bed."

A shiver ran through me at his words, but I straightened my spine, determined not to wimp out. Or rather, whimper, as his large and inviting bed stared back at me.

11

BILLIE

This time having Dylan in my room—in my bed—felt different. He looked pretty wiped, but pinpricks of heat licked over my entire body as we stripped to our boxers and fell into the soft sheets, barely giving each other a second glance. Bullseye had trouble getting up on the bed anymore unless I lifted him so I made him a spot on the floor near the headboard. Lately he'd been pacing in the middle of the night as if he couldn't quite get settled. But tonight he lay down immediately, most likely because it had been a busy day.

The room grew quiet as Dylan and I lay breathing side by side and the air felt thick with tension. But a couple of minutes later his breaths smoothed out and I figured he'd fallen asleep. I turned on my side to watch him by the light of the moon, but was surprised to find he was still awake, though his eyes were narrow slits.

He carefully twisted toward me on his pillow and we stared unabashedly at each other. He gazed at my mouth and into my eyes and I wanted to reach out and touch him so badly, my fingertips tingled.

I couldn't help wondering what his lips would taste like after his mouth had been on my neck and cock and I wasn't sure if he was thinking the same thing or if maybe he was wondering if this was a bad idea.

It was such a strange feeling thinking of him this way...but then, maybe it wasn't. We'd grown close over the years, worked every day together and lately, we'd done some intimate things I never would've dreamed of. So maybe this was only a natural progression. At least I told myself it was.

All at once Dylan's hand reached up to trace along my jaw and my heartbeat thundered in my ears. I held my breath as his fingers brushed over my cheek and forehead and then down to outline my lips. My chest pounded so hard that it ached with anticipation and visceral longing.

I thought back to those early days with Leo and how I was desperate for any kind of touch from him and this felt like the same kind of thing. Yet different. I was completely and utterly hot for my best friend, there could be no other explanation and I didn't know what the hell to do with that realization.

Not only because I had been saving myself for Leo, but because Dylan wasn't a person who took relationships seriously. Relationship? Listen to me. This was probably lust, plain and simple.

"You're going to make him happy," Dylan rasped as if reading my thoughts. His voice and words startled me in the still of the night and I grew even more motionless. "You'd make anybody happy."

My chest ballooned to a crescendo. "What about you?" I croaked out.

"What *about* me?" he asked, gently brushing the hair back from my forehead.

"Who would make you happy?" Even forming the words had somehow made my heart crack in pieces, but I couldn't quite understand why.

His breath stuttered as he stared hard at me. Finally, he said, "Me. I'll make myself happy. That's all I need."

My body ached so badly, I wanted to throw my arms around him and crush him with the weight of my yearning. I wanted to say, *Need me—please need me.*

Dylan hesitantly leaned forward and kissed my forehead. The feel of his soft lips nearly did me in. He lingered for a moment longer and then pulled back. "Good night."

When he settled into the sheets and closed his eyes, I watched him for what felt like an eternity, all kinds of emotions and sensations bombarding me at once.

I didn't know what finally made me do it but I sat up on one elbow and inched closer to him. I imagined fitting my mouth to his lips, my hands to his cheeks. My fingers ghosted his face like he'd done to me earlier.

Dylan's eyes sprang open. "What are you doing?"

"I...I don't know." My cheeks warmed to boiling point. "I just... you're so beautiful and I never realized it before."

His eyebrows knit together. "Gee, thanks."

"No, silly," I said with a laugh as his eyes narrowed comically. "I mean beautiful—inside and out. You're giving and loyal and decent. You need somebody to make you happy too."

The space between us filled with suffocating silence as we stared each other down. My chest felt so damn heavy it was as if my feelings and words were suspended in mid-air.

"*You* make me happy," he finally whispered with a sigh.

My chest rumbled and a low moan slipped out of my mouth.

Suddenly Dylan was right there; he clutched at my face, pulling me toward him. Our mouths melding as one, fitting together so perfectly.

He angled his head to fully seize my lips and he tasted like Dermot's sweet wine. When his fingers gripped my hair, he moaned. A moan that vibrated through my bones. His tongue slipped out to sample my lips and all at once it was inside my mouth, sweeping over my teeth and gums with deeply probing flicks. I melted into him, giving myself over completely to the sensation.

I adjusted my torso to position myself fully on top of him from heart to hip. As soon as our bodies aligned it was as if a live wire had been activated inside all of my nerve endings. Our penetrating kisses turned frantic and desperate as our hands explored and grasped and our legs tangled.

His fingers traced down my ribcage and beneath my waistband, stripping me of my boxers. My fingers blindly tugged his loose until we were finally skin to skin from our chests to our knees. And Christ, the feel of his hot and stiff cock resting heavily against mine nearly made me explode on contact.

"Holy fuck," I grunted against his mouth. His dick was long and thick and I wanted to see it. So damn badly.

"*Will*," Dylan mumbled, kissing my chin and throat and then up to my ear, his mouth searing my skin as he went. He pulled back, his fingers rushing down to encircle my cock. "Let me make you feel good."

"No," I gasped and he froze. "Not this time. I want to touch you. I need to fucking touch you."

I pushed away from his mouth and sat up to gaze into his warm eyes. They were glassy and full and I didn't know why he seemed so emotional, except that I was too. This was all too surreal.

But before I could overthink it, my hands went to work, touching every inch of him I could reach, from the top of his head down his chest and arms. Exploring his hips and legs and heels, appreciating his dancer's body as he trembled in the wake of my fingers.

I sucked his nipples into my mouth one by one, savoring his salty, spicy scent and as my tongue brushed over his stomach it convulsed. "Goddamn."

On my knees at his waist, I leaned over and licked the entire length of his dick, tasted his musk, savoring his velvet skin and the sensuous noises bursting from his throat. I circled the underside of the crown and then took him inch by glorious inch into my mouth, appreciating every last centimeter of his gorgeous cock.

Fuck, it had been way too long since I felt this way—eager and desperate to please somebody.

Dylan was grunting and gasping and his fingers were in my hair and brushing over the knobs in my spine. When his palm landed on my cheek he clutched and squeezed. It felt so sensuous to have somebody touch my ass again that I nearly arched off the bed. His fingers eased along the crease to my hole. My cock was leaking and so rigid I could pound nails with it. "Fuck, you're going to make me come."

"Good. It's mutual," he croaked and then I heard him suck on one of his fingers, getting it nice and wet.

As I continued lapping at him his hand was back in my crease and he prodded a finger against my hole. "So damn tight."

After my muscle loosened enough for him to push inside me, he began pumping in time with my mouth. When his digit curved up and hit my prostate, the room went fuzzy. I whimpered around his shaft as he hit that spongy place over and over again and I sucked him with all that I had.

"*Will.*" My name burst from his throat in one long syllable as his entire body shuddered and I felt his come coat the roof of my mouth. It was so fucking sexy that I could no longer hold back. His finger was still in my ass, my mouth engulfing his cock, and I came in a rush all over his thigh.

After another minute of inhaling roughly through my nose, I withdrew his softened cock from my lips and collapsed onto the sheets trying in vain to catch my breath. Holy fucking Christ.

He had reached for a shirt on the floor and wiped us up as I lay comatose beside him. "Billie, you...I..."

I was terrified of hearing the apology in his voice. Like he was going to play it off. Again.

"Please don't," I said and rolled over to sink into his warmth, my head in his neck. "Can you just hold me?"

His fingers against my chin, he tenderly kissed me, our lips and tongues sampling until we were so spent, we fell asleep with our foreheads resting together.

12

DYLAN

The following morning, Billie was tucked inside my arms and his heat was lulling me back to sleep. What happened between us last night felt distinctive from the other times. Like maybe Billie craved that intimacy with me and was struggling with his feelings about it.

I could see it in his eyes—the affection and the longing. And fuck, kissing him was like nothing I'd ever experienced. Uninhibited and profound at the same time. Like he had reached down into the deepest part of me and left a piece of himself there for safe-keeping.

I heard the murmur of voices out in the hall, which meant that the Montgomerys were rising to work the preserve on a Monday morning. I needed to get up as well, but it felt too good to be holding him, and if I moved even an inch, the spell might be broken. Reality might slap us in the face.

Nobody would bat an eye about our sleepover. It wasn't like I hadn't crashed here in the past. But this time felt different—almost clandestine. Especially after Billie's lips had been all over my body and remnants of my come were still in his mouth.

"What a pleasant surprise." Grammy's voice could be heard

from the kitchen. Showy and pitched, as if she were speaking loudly enough to rouse us awake. Or maybe just Billie.

Billie grew completely rigid in my arms—which meant he hadn't been asleep. Hopefully he hadn't lain awake for hours tormented by his decisions. Except he never broke free of my hold on him and he could've easily turned away from me.

"Sit and enjoy a fresh muffin, *Leo*," Grammy said, her voice carrying. "I'll see if Billie's awake."

Billie jackknifed to a sitting position, nearly giving me a bloody nose. "Leo's here. Why is Leo here?"

He rolled out of the sheets and stood up on unsteady legs. Realizing he was completely naked a blush rose from his chest to his neck to his cheeks. He stared down at me as if in awe. But then other emotions flitted across his face. Confusion and dread and excitement all rolled into one.

And even though my heart was cracking open, I understood it. This was Leo, his first love. The guy he'd been pining over for years. No matter what had happened between us, it wasn't something that was planned or could be figured out immediately.

Besides, we were only making each other feel good, right?

"Get going. Your boy is here to see you," I was able to muster out around the colossal boulder in my throat.

Billie stared at me for the longest moment, as he bit his lip and something like anger and sorrow flitted through his gaze. The same emotions I was feeling.

Finally, he nodded and began pulling on a T-shirt and shorts from his dresser drawer.

"I'll wait a few minutes," I said in a hollow voice. "So it looks like I slept in the guest room."

Billie ruffled his fingers through his hair—the same fingers that had been wrapped around my shaft just hours before—took a deep breath and reached for the knob. I was already sitting up and getting myself together, when he looked at me one last time and went out the door.

As I made my way to the bathroom down the hallway to take a leak and then head out on the road, I overheard part of their conversation from the kitchen entryway.

"A co-worker covered my shift for a couple of days, so I could come home." Billie had mentioned that Leo worked part time at a veterinarian's office. His life was perfectly scripted in a way that mine was not. "Sorry I missed the luncheon, but I couldn't get a flight out until last night."

"You probably deserve a break from all of those studies," Grammy said as my stride slowed. "You graduate in a couple of months?"

"That's right," he said. "Then I'm going to take a summer break at home before graduate school begins in the fall."

Billie had remained silent throughout that exchange and I wondered why. Was he still as shell-shocked as I was?

After I washed my face and finger-combed my hair, I unsteadily made my way to the kitchen, wishing I could escape any other way. As soon as I laid eyes on Leo I knew I could never measure up.

Whereas Leo was handsome and polished and accomplished, I was a high school graduate who danced in a club and helped my friend run his bakery. Even my best clothes from yesterday were wrinkled and purchased from a thrift store.

It made me want to escape this kitchen, this town, this life. Maybe I'd take Sebastian up on his offer and go to the city, maybe even search for some sort of job. I considered the exorbitant rent and the fact that I still needed food, shelter, and a livelihood and my shoulders slumped. Besides, I didn't even have a degree to stand on.

"Dylan, honey," Grammy said, spotting me and motioning me forward. "Glad you decided to stay in the spare room. I don't like you on the road so late." When my gaze met hers, there was a twinkle in her eye. She knew the other room was occupied. "Join us for some breakfast."

"You remember Dylan, right?" Billie said suddenly from his seat across the table. As if he'd just remembered his manners. He could barely hold eye contact with me.

"Of course," Leo replied and then reached out his hand for a shake. As our palms connected I couldn't purge the vision of my fingers tracing all over Billie's body.

I had pushed my way inside of him and made him come all over his sheets. *Me.* The country hick.

"Nice to see you. But I've got to take off. Cleaning out Mr. Brown's garage today," I mumbled just to have something to say. It was partially true. I did tell him I would help one of the next couple of weekends.

Bullseye was parked beside Billie's chair no doubt hoping for a table scrap and I bent down to pet him. "Hope you're feeling better today, buddy."

Leo asked Billie about Bullseye's hips and when the last time was that he'd been seen by his father, at the vet's office. He sounded so official, like he didn't still have years to go until he earned his license and I could taste the bitterness deep in my throat.

"Okay, see you later," I mumbled and pushed open the screen door like I was escaping from a house on fire.

"Dylan," I heard Billie call after me, but I was already down the steps. Nothing he said to me would make this scenario less awkward. When I slid in my front seat and looked back at the porch, Billie and Grammy were standing in unison at the screen door. Both had regret in their eyes so I mustered up a grin and a wave and got the hell out of there.

ALL MONDAY I kept myself busy with errands and Mr. Brown's garage and ignored Billie's texts.

I fished out the information Aaron had given me at STUDS

about auditioning for the upcoming production. I looked up the theatre online, and then drove an hour to the yellow brick building outside of Gainesville to fill out an application. Why I hadn't thought to do something like this myself a couple of years ago was beyond me.

I guess once I added up how pricey more college courses would be and how small the dance market was in the Roscoe area, I gave up. Besides, I had bills to pay to keep myself afloat. It had only been four years ago that I was living on the street and trying to make it through high school graduation. I needed to cut myself some slack.

I was told by the person at the front desk that I had just made the deadline and to return next Friday to audition in front of the judges. I felt good, accomplished, like I was doing something for me, even if I never made the production.

Aaron had thrown me a lifeline of sorts and I had grabbed hold of it with two hands. Had I never taken the job at STUDS, I would never have met him and sometimes baby steps were all you needed. So go put that in your pipe and smoke it, Billie.

But the truth was, at one time, Billie had also given me a life-line. Had I never spoken to him at lunch that one period our junior year to ask about his dog, I wouldn't be where I am today.

People come into your life for a reason, isn't that how the saying goes? And maybe all Billie and I would ever represent to each other is a period in our lives when we needed somebody to lean on and help through some tough circumstances. And probably it was time for both of us to move on. To make a clean break. Maybe we were using each other as crutches instead of standing on our own two feet.

But for now all I could do was take one day at a time.

When I showed up at Sweets on Tuesday for my regular workweek, Billie acted a bit miffed. "Way to respond to my texts."

"Sorry, I was busy—with Aaron," I said, for no good reason. "Remember, he helped me get that audition?"

I turned away from his probing eyes to start on the coffee machine as Billie's face turned beet red. But I told myself it was for the best. I needed to let him go so he could freely pursue Leo. I didn't want him to feel any regret or guilt. Leo was his dream just like dancing was mine.

The door to the café swung open with our first customers, and right behind the men who I recognized from the local lumberyard, was Leo. He walked in with a woman who was probably his mom, given her blonde hair and blue eyes.

"Wow," he remarked, looking around the space. "This place looks great."

It was as if he had materialized straight from my thoughts in order to remind me exactly why I was no longer needed.

13

BILLIE

As I served Leo and his mom my lemon meringue pie and told them about the new home superstore in town, I thought about what Dylan had said. About hanging out with Aaron. Had they finally hooked up? After he had been intimate with me?

What did it matter? I was ten kinds of confused anyway. It was great to see Leo. To spend some time with him yesterday. Our moments over the years had been too few and far between. We even made some definite plans to hang out this summer when he was home for a large chunk of time.

Still, things felt tentative between us, as if we were still feeling each other out. When we finally hugged goodbye after he had spend a good chunk of the morning out on the preserve, it was as if all of our memories from the past had rolled into one giant emotion and we clung to each other—either in nostalgia or despair.

But later that night, I could not get Dylan's arms out of my head. How I fit so easily inside them. How he knew exactly what I needed—how he always did these past couple of years.

And his lips and tongue. Damn. The way he kissed me with that quiet desperation made me ache all over again inside.

But despite how tenderly he always touched me in our intimate moments, he didn't want me outside of those times—not in that way. And I didn't want to lose his friendship. So I had to keep reminding myself of that fact even though his actions and words had totally thrown me. *You make me happy.*

Besides, I needed to consider how I feel having Leo around this week. When you hoped for something for so long and it materializes right in front of you, it's quite jarring and...different. Foreign. And I needed to ask myself why.

Had I put him on a pedestal like Dylan had told me I'd done all these years?

THE NEXT COUPLE of days I noticed how preoccupied Dylan was about his audition. He was also on his phone more than usual and I had to wonder if he was talking to Aaron.

He and I seemed to be walking on eggshells around each other and I was at a loss for how to get back to that middle ground between us—where we joked and ribbed and told each other practically everything. But now I was afraid of making a misstep or finding out something I did not want to hear.

Thursday night after we pulled the shades, locked the door and flipped the sign to CLOSED, I helped Dylan place the chairs up on the tables so he could sweep the floor.

"Can you show me?" I asked in a hesitant voice.

"Show you what?" he replied as he reached for the broom. It was the first time he had looked me directly in the eye in several long hours.

"Your routine for the audition." I handed him the dustpan. "I'd love to see it."

"What, here?" His gaze darted to the street as if somebody could see us. "I don't have enough—"

"When has that ever stopped you before?" I replied in a biting tone. I was tired of holding it all in. When my gaze met his in a challenge, he shook his head and laughed. All the tension slid from my shoulders as I grinned back at him. We'd finally broken through and found equal footing.

I leaned against the counter with my hand on Bullseye's neck, rubbing behind his ears while his tongue lolled in satisfaction. "*Please.*"

"Okay." He reached for his phone and searched for the right song.

He used the entire floor to dance to an up-tempo ballad with spins and grooves that I had never seen before. It was completely mesmerizing and I felt a strange twinge in my chest watching him so free and happy. When he was finished I clapped loudly and whistled.

"Holy crap, Dylan. It was gorgeous," I gushed. "*You* were gorgeous. That thing you did when you jumped in the air."

He was breathing heavily but his cheeks began to color from the compliment. "You think?"

"Yes," I said with enthusiasm. "You were made for the stage."

"Well, it's not much of a stage." He stooped over slightly to catch his breath. "And it's not like I was trained in any techniques."

"Hey," I placed my hand on his shoulder and I felt him stiffen momentarily. "You've got to start somewhere. Besides, that routine was pretty impressive for being self-taught. Have you never seen the *Step Up* movie?"

Hands on his knees he barked out a laugh. "Are you for real right now?"

"Two words. Channing Tatum." I folded my arms and narrowed my eyes. "You're full of shit if you say you've never fantasized about a hot celebrity."

"Of course I have. And he's definitely sexy," he said straightening his shirt. "But you'll never live that down. You better be nice to me or Callum is going to get an earful."

"Fuck you," I said, narrowing my eyes. "C'mon, when Channing was break dancing in the parking lot all hot and sweaty." I inched closer to him and his grin sobered as he sucked in a breath. "Just like you're drenched now. That's what made me think of it."

I reached forward and feathered my fingers through the damp hair near his ear. I felt a pang in my chest as our gazes connected for one drawn-out moment.

"Billie," he whispered. All at once there was a tap on the door. Shit, I had nearly forgotten about the new Marvel movie Leo and I were going to catch tonight. The theatre was in walking distance and I told him to show up around closing time.

I huffed out a breath as I removed my fingers from his skin. Dylan clenched his jaw, turned and headed to the door to let Leo inside.

When Leo stepped into the shop, he appeared to take in the room as his gaze swung between Dylan and me, a puzzled look on his face. "We're going to see a movie. Want to come?"

Dylan's gaze fell away as he mumbled, "No thanks. I actually have my own plans...with Aaron."

My stomach clenched as Dylan reached for his phone and bag before heading out the door. "Have a good night."

As I watched him leave through the kitchen, all I could think was how very much I missed my friend.

"Give me five minutes," I said, as I turned off the lights. Bullseye was already tucked away on his pillow near the door. "I thought about dropping him home. He'd be uncomfortable in the theater."

"Not sure you need to rely on him anymore, Billie," Leo said in a cautious voice, possibly remembering how important

Bullseye was to me and how vital he'd been in the early years of my disorder. "Seems like you're doing pretty well on your own."

"I know. He's just been such a fixture for so long." But the truth was, he was more a beloved family pet than a therapy dog anymore. I had outgrown him. My gaze met Leo's across the space and something niggled in my gut. In a lot of ways he was the same blond haired, blue eyed smart and beautiful boy I had fallen for. But I didn't have that same yearning for him. Not anymore. Maybe I had outgrown Leo, too.

"I'll pick you up in a couple of hours, buddy," I said, bending down and patting Bullseye's head. "Get some rest."

Bullseye didn't even budge as he snored away, content to finally be at rest.

The entire movie I was preoccupied with how graceful Dylan looked gliding across the floor and how disappointed I felt that he had plans with Aaron.

Leo and I shared popcorn and as our arms rested together during the movie, I didn't feel any sort of spark. In fact, more and more I realized that we didn't have much in common anymore. Maybe we never really did.

Ours was a young love where we only shared stolen moments in between him jetting off here and there to boarding school, college, or with his family. He'd always been more of an enigma than real to me. And maybe Leo had figured it out sooner than I had. He'd even said as much during our argument a couple years back in the city when he mumbled, "I'm not as perfect as you think I am." Guess I just wasn't ready to hear it.

After the movie, Leo walked me to the door of Sweets and waited as I opened it to call for Bullseye.

"Hey, buddy," I said stepping inside.

Bullseye lay heavy on his pillow, barely stirring. That was odd; he always greeted me without question, normally by hopping up and wagging his tail.

When I got closer, I patted his head and tried again. "Let's get you home."

With some effort, he opened his eyes and gingerly sat up only using his front paws for leverage.

When I looked back at Leo his eyes were laser focused on Bullseye's hind legs. "Try calling for him with a treat."

My heart jackhammering in my chest, I moved to the glass shelf to reach for a baked dog biscuit. "Want a treat?"

Bullseye's eyes perked up toward my outstretched hand, but he didn't move. "C'mon, boy."

He shifted his front feet forward, his back legs only dragged behind him.

"Stop," Leo said suddenly. "He can't move. Either his hips or his spine have given out."

"What do you mean?" I asked in a panic. "What's going to happen?"

He already had his phone out. "Help me carry him to the car and I'll call my dad to meet us at the vet center."

After he called his father, we worked in unison to slide a towel beneath Bullseye's body and then carried him to the car. He was panting openly in discomfort and he smelled like urine. Fuck, I had never seen him look so debilitated before.

I kept Bullseye as calm as I could in the back seat, but his sorrowful eyes seemed to be telling me something. He continued closing them every chance he got and I just kept rubbing his head not wanting to think of the consequences.

After we carried him into the vet's office, Leo's father thoroughly examined him using Leo as his assistant. Bullseye had his eyes closed the entire time and only wrenched them open when in pain.

Leo's father sighed heavily and looked my way. The moment before he said the words I knew what they were going to be and I braced myself for them.

"I'm afraid it's degeneration of his lower spine, which is

related to his dysplasia, and there's not much more we can do," he said in a soothing voice. "We can try to operate, but the success rate is low and he's at high risk under anesthesia. The humane thing to do—"

"Is to let him go," I finished for him as tears instantly sprang to my eyes.

"I'm sorry," he said and then turned to the door. "I'll give you a couple of minutes to think it through."

"It'll be okay," Leo said, after his father left the room. "We're here for you. Let me call somebody. Callum or Grammy. Maybe your dad?"

My answer came automatically. I knew exactly who I needed. "Dylan," I rasped through my tears. "I need Dylan."

My forehead sank down on top of Bullseye's snout and I sobbed my heart out.

"Hand me your cell. I'll ask him to come." Leo placed his hand on my shoulder, but it felt cold and foreign. Only Dylan's warmth would do.

14

DYLAN

When I got the call from Billie's phone it was Leo.

He quickly announced himself before saying, "Bullseye is gravely ill and Billie needs you."

My brain went on autopilot as I jumped up from my couch and ran out the door. "Where is he?" Leo told me they were at the vet center. My mind was going a million miles an hour. This would be killing Billie. I knew it would be and it was slaying me not to be there with him.

It felt like the drive took forever before I finally pulled into the parking lot.

After I got inside the exam room, and found Billie with swollen eyes holding a very sick Bullseye in his arms, my stomach bottomed out.

"I'm going to have to let him go," he said in a hoarse whisper.

"I know, baby. I know." He didn't even flinch when I stepped behind him and wrapped my arms around the both of them, a lump the size of the state of Florida in my throat. "He's not going to suffer anymore and that's a good thing."

"I'm glad for that," he said, twisting in my arms and burying his head into my neck. "I'm just going to miss him so fucking much."

I rocked him back and forth for several long seconds. Next time I looked up Leo stood in the entryway observing us with sorrowful eyes and I wondered if I had overstepped my bounds. But I didn't even care—I was only doing what felt natural. Taking care of my friend. The boy that I loved. The boy I'd do anything for, including swallowing my feelings so that he could be happy.

Leo cleared his throat and Billie simply burrowed further into my chest. "I called your family and they're on their way."

"Thank you," Billie said, wiping his eyes. I made the motion to back away, to allow for Leo to move in and take my place, but Billie only grabbed on firmer to my waist.

I had no idea why Billie was clinging to me so tightly except that I must've represented something he needed right then. Maybe consolation and a safety net and I wanted nothing more than to keep providing it for him.

After Grammy, Mr. Montgomery, and Billie's siblings showed up to comfort Billie and say goodbye, it felt like a funeral. But Bullseye was a part of their family, so it only seemed fitting.

"Will you please stay in the room with Bullseye and me when they—" Billie threw his arms around me, snuffling into my neck.

His entire body was rigid and unyielding, like he was terrified of what was to come. I felt a deep and bruising stitch in my chest, trying to keep my own emotions in check. "Of course."

The family waited in the lobby while I entered the room with Billie, Leo, and his father. A couple minutes after Billie said his final goodbye, Bullseye was given a shot of pentobarbital and put to sleep.

As the dog's eyes closed for the final time, I had never seen Billie cry so hard in my life. When I wrapped him in my arms, I attempted to stay strong but my own tears were blurring my vision.

Leo's dad told us that we'd be given the ashes in a couple of days' time so that we could bury him at Shady Pines. Billie mumbled that he'd like him to rest atop of Pines Ledge, in the shade beneath some evergreens.

When we stepped into the waiting room, Billie hugged his family one by one as they made their way out the door. "You got him?" Callum asked me.

"I'll make sure he has a ride home," I responded and he nodded solemnly, as he patted me on the back.

"Glad he has you," Grammy muttered and I looked around to see if she was in fact talking to me.

Billie was standing in the middle of the waiting room in a conversation with Leo. I heard him say that I would be driving him home and so I figured that Leo needed to hang back with his father to take care of the dog's remains. It had already seemed like he was his father's assistant during the procedure and I expected he'd make a good vet once he was licensed.

As Billie walked a few steps away to ask Leo's father a question, Leo nudged my arm. "I think Billie feels more than friendship for you and doesn't fully realize it yet."

As I shook my head in an attempt to respond, he continued. "No, it's okay. You're the only one he asked for when he had to make that decision. He wanted *you*, Dylan. I'm glad that you're in his life."

"But we're only—" I couldn't even make my mouth form the words, *just friends*. Not anymore.

Leo shook his head and our eyes met across the space. He knew I was only fooling myself.

"My life is really in Ohio now," Leo replied. "Plus I'll be headed back to graduate school. I'll always love him in my own way, but he needs somebody like you nearby."

I couldn't wrap my brain around what he was saying before he was walking Billie and me out the door. "Take good care of him."

When we got outside, Billie was unsteady on his feet, so I

helped load him in the truck. As soon as he slid into the passenger side, he crumpled against the seat. "Do you mind just driving around awhile?"

"Of course not." We rode through the countryside for a couple of hours simply listening to music or talking about Bullseye and how much he was a part of his life. All of our lives. You couldn't live in the town of Roscoe and not know Bullseye.

"Can I sleep at your place tonight?" Billie asked around a yawn. "I can't face my bedroom without him just yet."

I was nearly speechless. Billie hadn't been to my apartment very often because let's face it, it was a dump. When I didn't respond right away, he said, "*Please.*"

"That's cool. You don't have to go home," I said. "But, would you be more comfortable at Leo's house? I wouldn't mind—"

"No, I don't want...Leo's not...I just want to stay with you," he said in a rush. "If you don't want me, I can—"

"Of course I want you." *Fuck.* I reached for his hand on the seat and he interlaced our fingers, seeming relieved.

My stomach constricted so tight. Could Leo have been telling the truth about what Billie was feeling or was he just grieving so much that he was falling back on what was comfortable to him? No, I couldn't let my mind go there, not now, in the middle of all of this. I would be what my friend needed right now.

As soon as we got inside my apartment, I offered Billie some water, picking up some laundry as I went along. After downing a couple of glasses, using the bathroom to take a leak and wash his face, he followed me into the bedroom.

I got undressed and pulled back the sheets as he ripped his shirt off his shoulders, kicked out of his jeans and sank into bed, most likely fading from exhaustion.

I figured he'd fall asleep instantly, but his thoughts and emotions seemed to get the best of him. He tossed and turned for several minutes before finally throwing the covers off of him. "I just can't...."

"It's okay, let me hold you."

He scooted over into my arms and sank against me, releasing a more contented sigh. I rocked him and kissed the top of his head until he finally fell asleep.

A couple of hours later he lay awake again shifting positions and staring at the ceiling. I could hear his exasperated breath and feel the tension rolling off of him in waves. I tried to hold him again but he could not settle down.

"I want to kiss you again so badly," he said into my neck as I tried rearranging him against my chest. "But I don't want...if you and Aaron are..."

My mouth went dry. Holy Christ. "There is no me and Aaron."

He stilled. "There isn't? But you seem to be hanging out with him a lot."

I felt foolish now because I'd led him to believe something that wasn't true. "I wasn't. I just said that so that you didn't feel guilty being with Leo."

His eyes sprang up to mine. "Fuck, Dylan. I don't...I don't want Leo. I thought I did. I thought it with all my heart."

"What happened?" I whispered, attempting to dislodge the lump in my throat.

"I realized I wanted somebody else," he said. "I want *you*."

Holy fuck. Could this be for real or was that only his grief talking? "Billie—"

"No, don't. I can't analyze this...too much going on in my brain...just please kiss me. I need you to kiss me."

My heart was thrashing in my chest as I reached for his face, lined our lips and tenderly tapping our mouths together. But that didn't seem to be enough for him as he growled in frustration and smashed his mouth against mine.

His lips and hands grew feverish and almost punishing as he gripped my neck and nipped at my lips—as if he wanted to climb inside my skin to get closer to me.

He pushed me down on the bed and lay on top completely devouring my mouth.

Before I knew what was happening, he had both of our boxers on the floor and we were grinding against each other.

"I want you to fuck me," he growled in my ear.

"Goddamn, Billie," I panted against his cheek. "Hold up. I just don't think...I don't want you to regret anything."

He drew his head back to stare at me. His eyes were wild with longing and desperation. "What about you? Would you regret it?"

"Fuck no," I replied without a moment's hesitation.

"Then please," he pleaded, clutching at my jaw. "I need it...I need it so bad. I want to forget, if only for a few minutes."

After a long moment, I nodded, and then nudged at his shoulders. "Lie down."

As I rose up on my knees I figured it might destroy me if Billie woke up with remorse, realizing how needy and emotional he'd been.

But in this moment, I'd do anything for him.

15

BILLIE

I'd never felt such intense sadness in all my life. But behind that storm cloud of sorrow was also a ray of hope peeking through. I wanted Dylan so much. I wanted him on me and inside me, I wanted him to swallow me up and consume me. I wanted him to ball all of my pain into the palm of his hand and crush it into sawdust so I could truly appreciate the selfless beauty of him in this moment.

All of my nerve endings felt on fire as he kissed my skin with tongue and open mouth. From my throat to my collarbone down to my nipples which were overly sensitive tonight. All of my agony narrowed into a single pinpoint of light, like I was skating on the precipice of a knife and might catapult into the darkness if I got too close.

"Look how sexy you are, Will," he breathed into my abdomen as he licked and nipped at the skin. "I just want to devour you."

"Hell yes," I hissed as his chin bumped against my erection and he buried his nose in the patch of hair at my crotch.

His lips brushed down my length to my balls as I dug my heels into the mattress, feeling like I was only a hairsbreadth away from shooting all over myself.

"I love your cock and your balls," he muttered as he took his time sucking each one into his mouth. "I love how you smell. Like Sweets is in your blood, tattooed beneath your skin."

"Fuck," I moaned hoping like hell I could last long enough to feel him inside me.

He licked lower in broad strokes over my taint and then pushed at my thighs so that he could get better access to the crease of my ass. My knees shook as I lifted them to my shoulders and he kissed and licked my hole. My fingernails dug grooves into my flesh.

"Damn, I love tasting you," he murmured against my skin. "I could do this all night."

A groan tore from my throat. "*Please. I need more—*"

"You want my finger? I know how much you like that," he replied, circling a digit around my pucker.

"Yes," I hissed. He sat up to pull open a drawer on his nightstand, withdrawing a condom and some lube. He made quick work of squirting it on his fingers and my hole.

His tongue covered the distance to lap at my cock at the same time he pushed a finger inside. Stars floated in front of my eyes.

"Fucking hell." I writhed against him, all of my senses on hyperdrive as he drove in a second digit. "Oh damn. Please. I need you inside me."

He withdrew his fingers in order to roll on a condom as my chest heaved with raw anticipation. I could barely lie still—the urge to climb him like a tree was overpowering.

As he lined his cock up with my entrance, he leaned down to look me in the eye. "You sure about this?"

"I've never been more sure." I clutched at his face and fused our lips and tongues together, giving him everything I had, pouring all of my overwhelming emotions into the kiss.

"Fuck, Will," Dylan gasped against my lips. "Just...*fuck.*"

When he finally pushed inside me the searing pleasure-pain was the exact thing I'd been craving all along. It was as if I was suspended in a dreamland state of immeasurable bliss. Where nothing could hurt me. And nothing at all mattered except Dylan being buried deeply inside me, as his gaze carefully tracked my every response. He was so in tune to me—always had been—and I wondered if he even realized the profound emotions present in his eyes.

The tempo was slow and measured at first as if he needed to be careful with me. But he could tell the moment I became restless, my fists and jaw clenching, and began thrusting inside me with reckless abandon.

"Jesus, I always knew you would be good." He railed me hard as the headboard thumped in a steady beat against the wall. "But I never imagined this...oh fuck. *Unghhh.*"

"I can't even," I cried out, my spine on fire, my balls drawing up. "I'm not gonna last."

Eyes pinned to mine he reached for my cock with a solid grip. He didn't have to stroke too many times before I was shooting load after load over his hand and onto my chest.

My hole constricted around his cock and his jaw dropped open, his eyes glazed over and he came with a quiet sort of rumble that lifted all the fine hairs on my arms and legs.

When he finally collapsed on top of me, he pulled me into his arms and we rolled on our sides, our legs tangling, our mouths fused together. "Jesus, fuck."

I gasped into his neck as everything came crashing back in with an unwavering intensity that rocked me to my core.

Bullseye's death. Letting Leo go. Falling for my best friend.

As the raw emotions seared straight through me, the only thing holding me aloft was Dylan's arms. As if he were keeping me caged, contained in his warmth—and if he ever let go, I'd be drifting away and lost again.

After our heart rates evened out, I swiped carelessly at my torso with some Kleenex that Dylan had handed me from his nightstand, as he tied the condom and tossed it on the floor. I felt

Dylan's shoulders relax and I knew that he had drifted off to sleep. It had been one hell of a long night.

Still, I had trouble settling down, my mind restless and troubled with so many flickering thoughts and feelings. As I watched Dylan sleep, I couldn't stop the words from tumbling from my mouth. I needed to get them out even though he was barely conscious.

"I've fallen in love with you, Dylan." My fingers brushed over his curls at his forehead. "I know you probably don't want to hear that because...well, I'm your friend and you don't really do relationships."

My lips quivered as I relaxed against my pillow and talked to the ceiling. "But I also wonder if maybe you're afraid because you've had a lot go wrong in your life. You've had plenty of people shit on you. Maybe you're terrified of being on the losing end again."

I shut my eyes, my heart rate finally decelerating as I forced the final words out. "I'm afraid too. Mostly of losing you. But if I don't take this gamble and finally tell you how I feel, I might waste the chance of having something great with one of the best people I know. Because, fuck. You're strong and faithful and absolutely *stunning*."

I draped my arm over his torso as I began drifting into a quiet slumber. "I mean, look at you..." I mumbled. "You're...*everything*."

16

BILLIE

A few hours later, I padded out of the bedroom in only my boxers careful not to wake Dylan and reached for my phone on the coffee table.

I sat down on the couch and noticed a text from Callum telling me to take the day. That he and Dean would go to town to check on Sweets. It sounded liked a perfect plan, at least for the morning, because I still needed to gather this tornado of emotions inside of me.

After I responded to Callum, thanking him, I steadied my breath and dialed Leo.

"Everything okay?" he asked the second he picked up.

I inhaled through my nose. "It will be."

"You're with Dylan?"

I hesitated, my pulse quickening. "I am."

"You're in love with him."

Damn, he already knew. But how could he not after I asked for Dylan above anybody else? "I...I'm sorry."

"No need to be," he replied. "I actually think it's really great. It's the way it should be."

I leaned back and stared at the celling, relief and anxiety

coursing through me. "Yeah, I just don't know if he—"

"He needs you as much as you need him," he said with a smile in his voice, as if he already had it all figured out. "It'll all be okay, you'll see."

I swiped at the tear rolling down my cheek with a shaky hand.

"Thanks, Leo. For yesterday and a bunch of other things over these past few—"

"No need to thank me. Just live your life...and be happy."

It was the same sentiment from the letter he'd written four years back and now it all came full circle. As it turns out, I was living my life. I was pretty happy. I just hadn't realized it.

There was a long pause as if a rope were dangling between us that needed to be severed. And then it finally was. "Goodbye, Leo," I said, in a strangled whisper.

"Take care, Billie."

I hit the button to end the call and stared hard at my phone. It was the sweetest kind of goodbye. One filled with equal parts hope and melancholy.

Right then Dylan padded out of the bedroom in a pair of sweats and sank down beside me on the couch. He propped his feet on the table and mumbled something about making coffee.

"Was that Callum?" he asked, rubbing the sleep out of his eyes.

"Leo." I felt him stiffen beside me.

I sighed and propped my feet next to his. "I've said some tough goodbyes the past twenty-four hours."

His body melted further into the cushions as his gaze landed squarely on mine.

"I know." He patted my knee, and kept his warm fingers there. "You don't have to say goodbye to *me*."

I shut my eyes as profound relief coursed through all of my limbs. "No?" I mumbled.

"For the record, I *am* afraid," he said and I gasped, my lids springing open. "Afraid of losing you. Was too chicken to open my eyes last night for fear it all might've been a cruel fucking dream."

I remained silent because I didn't want to miss one single thing he had to say. Instead, I placed my hand on top of his and interlaced our fingers.

"Afraid that I probably feel *way too much* for my best friend."

My heart rose to my throat. "*Impossible.*"

"You pain in the ass," he said with a chuckle and then yanked on my hand so that I could nuzzle against his chest. His lips resting at my temple made me sigh.

He wrapped his strong arms around me and pulled me further into his sleepy warmth.

"I...need to go home and face it," I muttered into his neck. "Face Bullseye being gone."

He nodded. "Want me to—"

"No, not this time." I pulled back to gaze at him. "I need to do it on my own. Think I've been using him as a crutch—a lot of things in fact—and even he probably knew it."

"Nah, he just knew you were his human." His fingers brushed beneath my chin. "The one person he'd stick around for through anything. You were so good to him."

When he stared hard into my eyes it was as if he were talking about himself and not my faithful dog.

I felt tears pricking my eyes again. "Will you help me bury him?"

"Absolutely."

I swiped at my face with my forearm and considered my years of pining over Leo, as well as some grudges I'd been holding against important people in my life who mattered so much and only meant well. "Guess it's time to let go of childish notions."

"And time for me to get my ass moving. Grab hold of my dreams," he murmured.

I nearly sprang off the couch. "Holy shit, your audition."

He waved me off. "It's not a big deal."

"Of course it is," I said, swatting him playfully. "You have to go. It's a start."

A small smile lined his lips. "A start to what?"

"Going after what you want in life."

He gathered my face in his hands. "I want *you*, does that count?"

"It counts very much," I whispered against his lips. "Does that mean you also want—"

"Everything?" He grinned before pecking my lips. "Of course. I love you, Billie. I have for a long time."

I blinked, realization dawning on me. I grabbed hold of his jaw and kissed him breathless. Morning breath be damned.

"Can you do me a favor?" I asked nuzzling his ear.

"Anything."

"Can you start calling me Will—like, all the time?"

"I knew you got a boner for that."

I smacked him hard and he tackled me to the couch. Straddling me, he said, "First you're going to tell me you love me again. I'll need to hear it every day, by the way."

He lightly ticked my sides and I laughed. "I love you, you fucker. Now get the hell off of me."

"Not until we get some other things straight."

I grew motionless and looked him in the eye. I didn't mind feeling his weight on top of me and he knew it too. Still, I folded my arms in protest. "Go on."

"I'm going to the audition and you're going to be with your family and probably say some more goodbyes."

My eyes filled with unshed tears and he swiped at the imaginary wetness on my cheeks.

"And then maybe later," he continued, softening his voice, "we can look at the calendar and plan our road trip."

My eyes grew wide and I nearly squealed. "Seriously?"

"Yeah," he said and scooted back on the couch. "Now get your ass moving. We've got some living to do."

17

DYLAN

"I'm proud of you, son." Mr. Montgomery braced Billie's shoulder and I noticed how he had relaxed into his touch. "Proud of you both."

My heart stuttered a little in my chest as Dean nudged me and winked.

The entire Montgomery family was standing on top of Pines Ledge, their gazes beneath the evergreen tree where we'd buried Bullseye's ashes—looking over the Shady Pines property, like a protector of the land.

Callum had constructed a small wooden marker, with his name burnished into it, along with his birth and death years, and then sealed it with some sort of special coating so it wouldn't rot out here in the elements.

"Thank you, sir," I sputtered barely able to get any coherent words out. Billie's father had always been a strong, silent and somewhat imposing figure in this family and though I knew I was always welcome, he'd only spoken to me directly on a few occasions. Once was early on when he'd called my dad a "good for nothing" and other choice words before he grumbled about me getting something decent to eat in the kitchen with Grammy.

It'd been a small feat for Grammy to make it up the incline to the Pines Ledge lookout point this warm afternoon, but she was a trooper. As she took Braden's arm and clutched her walking stick, she said, "We'll see you back at the house. Dinner will be ready soon. *Will's* favorite."

When I saw the gleam in her eye, I grinned. "Wouldn't miss it."

She'd told Billie and me on numerous occasions the past few days how thrilled she was that we'd found our way to each other. The rest of the family appeared to share the sentiment, which eased my mind. It was one thing to be Billie's best friend, quite another to make the leap to boyfriend status.

After Cassie kissed Billie's cheek, Braden thumped his back, and Callum gave him a bear hug, the family walked down the path in unison, knowing Billie needed another quiet minute to officially say goodbye.

As I watched them hike down the rocky path, it was strange not to see Bullseye beside them as a living and breathing fixture after all these years, but he'd had a good life with this wonderful family.

Billie and I settled against a large rock, and as I kissed his temple, he swiped away a leftover tear. I had been nervous about him all week, wondering if he was getting enough sleep and if he'd relapse as a result. But Grammy had invited me to stay a few nights in the "guest room" in order to help him through his grief.

A couple days back during one of his lowest moments, I had asked if he wanted to bring home a new puppy, but he refused. "Besides, we've got plans," he'd said, with a hopeful glint in his watery smile.

I had found out just yesterday that I'd made the cast of *Hairspray* and rehearsals were to begin in a couple weeks' time, which meant between Sweets and the production, I'd be plenty busy. But I'd never felt so settled and happy in my life. I'd decided to finish out the month at STUDS if only to save more money for those plans Billie was referring to. But kissing for more tips would be strictly off-limits. Besides, I didn't want anybody else's mouth or hands. Billie was it for me.

"Got a message from Sebastian," I said, removing my phone from my pocket and scrolling through the thread. I'd been texting quite a bit lately with him and Tate. I felt strangely connected to them for some reason. "He said they'd love to have us visit this fall."

We'd decided to drive east on our road trip this time around and New York City was going to be one of our stops.

"Awesome," Billie replied, and then stared down at the grave, maybe wondering how it would feel without Bullseye. There had been a lot of changes in his life recently and he'd need time to process it all. Same as me.

The shade felt nice as we sat silently for several minutes staring off into the distance. Billie grinned at the faint gong of the dinner bell that had been in the family for over a hundred years. Grammy was letting the Montgomerys know that they needed to get their butts to the supper table. You didn't mess with Grammy.

I walked over to Bullseye's grave and squatted down, patting the wooden marker.

"I'll take good care of him, Bullseye. I promise."

I heard a strangled whimper from over my shoulder as Billie's eyes filled with unshed tears and he knelt down beside me. "You always have, Dylan. I love you so damn much."

My heart vaulted to my throat as I pulled him into my arms and kissed his neck and ear and forehead. "I love you, too. Always have. Always will."

After we kissed tenderly for another long moment, Billie stood up, brushed off his knees and held out his hand. "You ready?"

I nodded and interlaced our fingers as he pulled me up. "I better be or Grammy's going to have something to say about it."

Billie's laugh echoed through the pine trees and the sound

was so pure and warm that it reached that place deep inside me reserved only for him.

"Let's go *home*," Billie said, tugging at my arm.

I felt a winging in my chest as my heart flapped and fluttered at his words. "Sounds perfect."

The idea of a warm, safe and familiar place to finally call my own never felt more real—or more right.

THANK YOU for reading THE SWEETEST GOODBYE!

I hope you enjoyed it!

Reviews help other readers find books. So if you feel compelled one way or another to leave a sentence or two on a retail site, I appreciate it!

Read on to view a short excerpt from book one in the Under My Skin Series, REGRET!

ABOUT THE AUTHOR

Once upon a time, **Christina Lee** lived in New York City and was a wardrobe stylist. She spent her days getting in cabs, shopping for photo shoots, eating amazing food, and drinking coffee at her favorite hangouts.

Now she lives in the Midwest with her husband and son—her two favorite guys. She's been a clinical social worker and a special education teacher. But it wasn't until she wrote a weekly column for the local newspaper that she realized she could turn the fairy-tales inside her head into the reality of writing fiction.

She's addicted to lip balm and salted caramel everything. She believes in true love and kissing, so writing romance novels has become a dream job.

OTHER TITLES BY CHRISTINA LEE

Standalone:

Love Me Louder

There You Stand

Beautiful Dreamer

MMM with Felice Stevens:

Last Call

First Light

Under My Skin series

Regret

Reawaken

Reclaim

Redeem

Co-written with Nyrae Dawn (AKA Riley Hart):

Free Fall series:

TOUCH THE SKY

CHASE THE SUN

PAINT THE STARS

Spinoff from Free Fall series:

LIVING OUT LOUD

Standalone:

EVER AFTER: A GAY FAIRY TALE

AN EXCERPT FROM REGRET

BRIN

I pushed the key in the lock at Doggie Styles, securing the glass entrance for the night. My co-worker Elijah had cashed out our last dog—a cute-but-yippy schnauzer—on the grooming side but I was stuck on the daycare end waiting for the final pickup. Elijah had already asked for my Chinese takeout order before hitting the road, letting me know I'd see him within the hour. I took a deep breath and headed to my Volkswagen, where more of my clothes were piled sky high in the back seat.

My life had been running smoothly for far too many weeks in a row, and I knew something was bound to fuck it up. So when I'd stepped foot inside my condo a couple nights back and my feet sloshed in the standing water from the burst pipe covering every square inch of my cozy place, I figured the time had come. This was why I couldn't have nice things. Not even a respectable boyfriend for fuck's sake, which is why I finally deleted my Tinder account weeks ago. Time to finally get my shit together, and this setback was a definite reminder.

Elijah had offered for me to stay on the futon in his home office until my place dried out and the flooring was replaced. When I'd walked into my bedroom to retrieve some basic necessities yesterday, giant industrial fans had been set up to help with the task. But the floor still squished as I walked, and the condo was beginning to smell musty. Fuck my life.

Thankfully, my collection of Marvel and DC comics had been on the highest shelf in my closet, so the water had never reached the box. Most of them had come from my Uncle Rick who'd died from AIDS when I was ten years old, so they had become one of my most prized possessions. Now they were safely tucked away in the trunk of this car.

I'd definitely miss the creature comforts of my condo but was glad for the helping hand. I supposed I could've stayed with my parents on the east side the entire month, which would've been a hike to work every day. But quite honestly, the blank expression on my father's face the last couple of nights—along with the obvious tension around his eyes—made me accept Elijah's offer in about one second flat. Mom always tried to smooth the distant relationship between my father and me, but I didn't think I could hack it for one more day.

I slid onto the black leather seat, glad my Jetta was still in decent shape, and if I had wood to knock on, I'd definitely take advantage. As it was, I'd already spent most of the day on the phone with the insurance company as they assessed the loss. According to the claims agent all of the damage should be covered, so that was one good thing that came out of this. Even if it put me out for weeks on end.

As I drove the back streets from Rocky River to Clifton Avenue in Lakewood, it reminded me how much I liked this neighborhood with its century-old homes located in close proximity to Lake Erie. Elijah lived in a quaint and spacious building with a roommate who'd been out when I was dropping off the majority of my stuff yesterday. I'd be sleeping in their spare bedroom-turned-office, and it felt comfortable enough as I waited for my condo to be repaired. Besides, no way I'd want to be a pain in the ass houseguest when I was the one imposing on them.

I had never met Nick, but I'd be sure to thank him and apologize for any inconvenience my staying there might cause. Elijah would tell me I needed to stop saying sorry for every damn thing in life and then I'd roll my eyes and remind him that I was a work in progress. Apologizing for who I was and what I needed just seemed to be my life's mission.

I finally found a place to park on the busy road, which would become a pain after a few days' time. Both Elijah and his roommate paid extra for space in the parking garage. That was the way to go if you wanted to live on an active street close to a busy intersection lined with several stores and restaurants.

Lifting the hangers from the back seat, I gently draped the clothes over my arm before twisting to slam the door shut. Pushing apartment two-oh-two on the board, it took Elijah several seconds to buzz me up. He stood with the door ajar when I got up the second flight of stairs. Knowing I needed to head straight for the office before my arm got numb, he simply followed behind me past the bathroom to the tiny third bedroom.

"Think you're all set now?" he asked as I slid the closet door open with one hand and then lifted the hangers from my other arm.

"Yeah," I replied, lining the T-shirts in a mostly neat row before sliding the door shut again. "If I need any more toiletries, I'll just buy them."

"Good plan." Elijah glanced over his shoulder when we heard two more voices—one of which I suspected was his roommate.

"Nick just got home with Sarah," he said with a smirk. And then whispered, "His newest *friend*."

The only thing I'd heard about Nick over the past year was that he was a cool guy, always busy, and dated his share of women. I was suddenly glad Nick and Elijah's bedrooms were on the other side of the apartment and the kitchen and living room separated us.

Elijah also made sure to mention that Nick was hot as fuck but wouldn't dare state that fact in front of his boyfriend, Stewart, who could be a jealous prick, not that I'd ever tell Elijah that completely sober.

I sort of wondered if Nick felt the same, since Stewart was bound to stay over quite a bit. Obviously, Nick had to be mostly cool with the arrangement or Elijah would've mentioned it. Although, maybe not. He blabbed about every damn thing, except when it came to his relationship with Stewart, which he considered sacrosanct.

"Brin, let me introduce you to my roommate," Elijah said as I followed him through the short hallway to the living room. "This is Nick and his *friend*, Sarah."

Sarah's curly locks were nearly as blond as mine and Nick's black hair was mostly tucked beneath a worn blue baseball cap. The two of them were cozy on the couch, Sarah sitting with her legs tucked under her and Nick with his ankle crossed over his knee. They were eating Chinese food off paper plates resting in their laps. Sarah simply waved as her mouth was full from a bite of food but Nick responded, "Hey, how you doing?" after swallowing a piece of what looked like an egg roll.

The smell of fried rice hit my nostrils and when my stomach rumbled in response, I realized just how famished I was. I was dying to dive right into the second brown bag resting on the coffee table that more than likely contained my food, but I didn't want to be rude.

When Nick leaned forward with an outstretched hand, for some reason I zeroed right in on the neatly groomed scruff on his chin. When he tilted his face to look directly into my eyes, I froze, our fingers interlocked. A startled gasp sprang from my lips, and Nick's eyebrows slammed together in confusion right before they lifted straight to his hairline.

The same cherry-colored lips, with a center dimple drilled into his chin. Those sad, amber-colored eyes that shuttered out the world.

Holy fuck. Elijah's roommate was Nicholas Dell.

The same Nicholas Dell from Jefferson High who practically ruined me for other guys.

The same Devil's third baseman that begged his math tutor to suck his cock in the locker room after practice.

And given the female nestled up beside him, it was the same Nicholas Dell who was still deep in the closet.

Made in the USA
Middletown, DE
19 February 2023